LONG BOMB

Eric Howling

James Lorimer & Company Ltd., Publishers
Toronto

James Lorimer & Company Ltd., Publishers acknowledges funding support from the Ontario Arts Council (OAC), an agency of the Government of Ontario. We acknowledge the support of the Canada Council for the Arts, which last year invested $153 million to bring the arts to Canadians throughout the country. This project has been made possible in part by the Government of Canada and with the support of Ontario Creates.

Cover design: Gwen North
Cover image: Shutterstock

Library and Archives Canada Cataloguing in Publication

Title: Long bomb / Eric Howling.

Names: Howling, Eric, 1956- author.

Series: Sports stories.

Description: Series statement: Sports stories

Identifiers: Canadiana (print) 2019018650X | Canadiana (ebook) 20190186518 | ISBN 9781459414846 (softcover) | ISBN 9781459414853 (EPUB)

Classification: LCC PS8615.O9485 L66 2020 | DDC jC813/.6—dc23

Published by:
James Lorimer &
Company Ltd., Publishers
117 Peter Street, Suite 304
Toronto, ON, Canada
M5V 0M3
www.lorimer.ca

Distributed in Canada by:
Formac Lorimer Books
5502 Atlantic Street
Halifax, NS, Canada
B3H 1G4

Distributed in the US by:
Lerner Publisher Services
1251 Washington Ave. N.
Minneapolis, MN, USA
55401
www.lernerbooks.com

Printed and bound in Canada.
Manufactured by Marquis in Montmagny, Quebec in December 2019.
Job #181200

For Duncan, and the cool Mustang he drove in high school.

Contents

1 One of the CROWD

The stands were rocking.

The game wasn't scheduled to start until four o'clock but the Wednesday afternoon crowd was already cheering. Hands were clapping. Feet were stomping. Mouths were shouting. The fans from Calgary High couldn't wait for the opening kick-off to watch their Mustangs play the Central Chargers.

I hiked up the stands, taking two steps at a time. When you're skinny as a giraffe and pushing six-foot-four at fourteen, it's the only way you can climb stairs.

As a little kid I had always loved football. I couldn't wait for the weekends when Dad would take me to play in the park. I wasn't very tall then, but I knew I wanted to be a great pass receiver just like Dad was in college. He would throw passes to make me better. Sometimes, he'd throw the ball really high and I always caught it. Then he told me a secret. That catching a really high pass was good because the defender couldn't reach it. He couldn't stop you from making

7

the grab. Dad and I did that for years and I got pretty good. Then one day, it all ended. It's hard to play catch when your dad leaves town and doesn't come back.

I didn't play football after that. But it was just as well. I wouldn't have been a very good player. At twelve I started to shoot up and I didn't stop. Mom could barely keep up measuring me against the back of my bedroom door. She always said, "Ed Warnicki, you're growing like a weed!"

Being tall and thin isn't such a good thing in football. All it would take is one crunching tackle and I'd be snapped in half. Watching from the stands was as close to wearing a Mustangs uniform as I was going to get.

I found a seat a few rows up and folded my long legs under the bench. Sitting by myself didn't bother me. I sat alone in most of my classes anyway. It wasn't like I was Mr. Popular or anything — not like the guys who played on the football team. But being close to the action made me feel part of the game. I could even hear Coach Taylor shouting to his players on the Mustangs sideline.

A line of green uniforms spread across the field, set for the Calgary kick-off. The Central return man made the catch and ran the ball back. He was a red streak sprinting straight up the middle of the field. He darted all the way to the Central forty-yard line before our Mustangs tackler could bring him down. The Chargers fans cheered but it wouldn't last long. Disaster struck on their first play from scrimmage.

"Fumble!" Coach Taylor yelled from the Mustangs bench. He pointed at the loose ball squirting across the grass. The Chargers running back had coughed up the pigskin and a Calgary linebacker had jumped on it. The Mustangs defence charged off the field after the fumble recovery, pumping their fists.

Coach Taylor barked out orders to his players. "Jackson! Offence! Let's go!"

The Mustangs ran onto the field. That's when the crowd really went nuts.

"There he is!" a girl shouted, jumping to her feet three rows below me.

Other hands shot out, pointing at number twelve in the green uniform trotting onto the field.

"Touchdown, here we come!" a guy yelled, his hands cupped around his mouth.

Everybody had been waiting for the Mustangs star quarterback. Tyrone Jackson was big and strong and had a powerful arm. I could see why people thought he was the best QB in the league. But I had heard other stories too. Like that his temper was as big as his talent.

I watched number twelve go to work. After calling a play in the huddle, Tyrone crouched over his centre and shouted out signals, waiting for the snap. He faked a pass then smoothly handed off the ball to his running back. Levi Wilson broke outside the Central cornerback and sprinted down the sideline for twenty yards before being tackled. The ball was in Chargers territory on the thirty-yard line. First down, Mustangs.

The crowd exploded.

"Come on, Tyrone, you can do it!" another girl shouted. "You can do anything!"

Tyrone's next call fooled everybody, including me. I thought he'd try another running play. But this time he took the snap and faked a hand-off. Then he dropped back a few steps to pass. He looked far down-field and spotted a Mustangs wide receiver breaking into the clear. Tyrone pulled his arm back and fired a bullet. The ball spiralled though the clear blue sky, and right into the receiver's hands. Lamar Williams caught the brown leather then beat the only defender between him and the goal line. Lamar had the best jets on the team.

The ref shot both arms up over his head — touch-down! Tyrone raced into the end zone and high-fived Lamar. The Mustangs players mobbed their receiver and cheered on the field. The Mustangs fans high-fived each other and cheered in the stands. The Calgary kicker booted the one-point convert. The Mustangs had taken the lead, 7–0.

2 The NEXT GUY

I shook my head after watching Lamar's amazing play.

I wondered what it must be like to be a Mustang. To be a star receiver like Lamar. To catch a big touchdown pass.

Coach Taylor patted Tyrone on the back when he came back to the bench. "Lucky you saw Lamar was open!"

"Luck had nothing to do with it, Coach." Tyrone shook his head. "I've got the best arm in the league. Every pass I make is perfect."

I didn't know if Tyrone Jackson could throw better than any other quarterback in the league. But I did know he had the biggest ego in the league.

The Mustangs defence forced the Chargers to punt the ball, and Tyrone rushed back onto the field. I doubted whether he could repeat his great play. I was sure no one could be that good.

I was wrong.

Tyrone first called another running play. He handed

off the ball to Levi, who was built short and round like a bowling ball. Levi rolled through the Chargers defensive line as if he was knocking down a bunch of pins. He gained twenty yards for a first down.

Next play Tyrone showed off the power of his arm. The Chargers had called a blitz. Their speedy cornerbacks came charging across the line as soon as Tyrone took the snap. They chased him out of the pocket their big defensive linemen had formed to protect their quarterback. Tyrone knew what to do. He scrambled away from the rushing players and looked downfield. He spotted Lamar in the clear and launched a long pass while he was still running at full speed.

Lamar snagged the throw with both hands, then held the football in one arm to make it easier to run. He raced down the sideline and bolted into the end zone. He spun the ball on the ground to celebrate the score. Another touchdown for Lamar. Another high-five from Tyrone.

The cheerleaders jumped into action. The crowd leaped to its feet.

"It's high-school football but we have a pro quarterback!" shouted a short guy with zits. "Tyrone is my man!"

"Give it up, Central!" yelled a cute girl behind me. "This game is over!"

And it was. The Mustangs continued to dominate

the game. When the referee blew his half-time whistle, Calgary was leading 21–0.

Tyrone jogged back to the Mustangs bench. He took off his helmet and wiped his sweaty forehead. It was a hot September afternoon and the sun beat down on the field. "Where's my water bottle?" Tyrone yelled as he looked around for the waterboy. "I need a drink."

He didn't have to look far. Just a few steps away, a boy stood staring at his phone.

"Hey, bro, is your job checking Facebook or checking to make sure all these water bottles are filled for the players?" Tyrone had his hands on his hips.

"Sorry, Tyrone." The boy ran over to the cooler and started to fill the bottles. He looked panicked and more water splashed out than went in. "Won't happen again."

"You got that right," Tyrone snarled. "You don't deserve to be part of the Mustangs team. Give me that drink and take a hike."

The boy finished filling Tyrone's bottle then skulked off like a whipped dog.

After the third-quarter kick-off, the Mustangs continued to roll up the score. The Chargers were outclassed in every way. They weren't as fast, as big or as tough as the team with the green uniforms. Our Mustangs were putting on an awesome display of power. By the end of the game, Tyrone had thrown another touchdown pass to Lamar and handed off the ball to Levi for one more. The final score was Mustangs 35, Chargers 7.

The crowd was still buzzing over the win as I followed the happy fans streaming down the bleacher steps. When I neared the bottom, I could hear a heated conversation taking place on the field. Tyrone was standing by the water table. "I even had to get my own drink," he complained to Coach. "Where is that little water weasel?"

"He quit." Coach eyed his star quarterback. "Said something about getting hassled by a player. You wouldn't know anything about that would you, Tyrone?"

"Now what are we going to do?" Tyrone threw up his hands. "The season has already started. We'll never find another waterboy now. Maybe we should just hire the next guy we see." Tyrone glanced up into the stands. That's when our eyes locked.

"Hey, you!" Tyrone said.

"Who, me?"

"Yeah, you, string bean. Want to be the new waterboy for the Mustangs?"

I stared blankly at the big quarterback. I had never thought about being a waterboy. I had only thought about being a player. But every time I thought about playing, I'd take a look at my skinny arms and toothpick legs and forget about it. Plus, I was already busy working after school at the 7-Eleven. Would I even have time to be a waterboy?

But this was the Mustangs. If I could never play for them, at least I could be their waterboy.

"Yeah . . . sure."

"Then you start right now." Tyrone waved me down to the field. "Get over here and clean up this mess."

3 SNACKS

I could hear the music even before I saw the car. Heavy bass pounded through the air as the powerful machine pulled in front of the store. My Wednesday night shift at 7-Eleven had just started. I stood slouching behind the cash register.

This could be trouble, I thought.

A quick glance out the window told me everything I needed to know. The car was a green Mustang. That could only mean one thing — it was the star of this afternoon's football game, Tyrone Jackson.

Tyrone's dad owned the local Ford car dealership. The whole school knew he had just given Tyrone a new car for his sixteenth birthday. And not just any car — a brand new Mustang custom painted the same bright green as the Mustangs uniforms. I had to admit it was a sweet ride.

The front door of the store swung open. Tyrone breezed in with Jerry Fishburn and Zara Kapoor. Tyrone and Zara were holding hands, so I was pretty sure they were an item. Their eyes darted across the aisles and the trio quickly headed down one of them. I could tell they were on a mission to find snacks. You didn't have to be a rocket scientist to find them at this store — they were on every shelf.

"Over here!" Tyrone called out, excited by his discovery. "I knew we could find them."

Jerry grabbed a bag of Doritos and grinned. "I could eat these all day."

His real name was Jerry Fishburn but everyone called him Fish for his last name and round bulging eyes. His claim to fame was being Tyrone's sidekick. Everywhere Tyrone went, Fish swam right along beside him. Fish was a smooth talker and would set up Tyrone with jokes so that he looked good in front of his classmates — mainly the girls. Fish was small as a guppy with a few red zits peppering his oily face. But Tyrone didn't mind because having Fish beside him all the time made him look bigger, stronger and better looking.

"Tyrone, your party on Friday night is going to rock," Zara said. Her big brown eyes beamed up at him.

There were always lots of house parties in September after kids came back from vacation. Everyone wanted to find out what kind of summer jobs people had, how dark their tans were and how much taller they had grown. Even I had added another two inches to my stickman frame. Not that I needed it.

Long Bomb

Zara liked to play the party girl. She had a purple streak running through her black, spiked hair. The small butterfly tattoo on her neck made her seem tough. But I knew Zara was a lot smarter than she let on. She was fifteen and had already skipped a year. Not only that, she was the editor of the school paper, the *Mustang News*. So she was pretty much a brainiac.

"I can't reach it!" Zara called from the back of the store. "Help me, Tyrone!"

"I'm busy," Tyrone called back, eyeing some Pringles. "Ask that bag of bones behind the counter."

Zara was standing in front of the drink cooler, pointing at a bottle of Coke on the top shelf. "That one," she said when I approached. Her outstretched hand didn't even reach as high as my head.

I opened the cooler door and easily grabbed the bottle for her. "Here you go."

"Thanks. At least someone is willing to help me." Zara shot a sideways glance at Tyrone in the next aisle. If Tyrone and Zara were a couple, they sure had a funny way of showing it, I thought, returning to the cash register.

A minute later the three party shoppers were standing in front of me. A mountain of snack bags spilled out of their arms. Potato chips, corn chips, popcorn, pretzels, Reese's Pieces, two boxes of Oreos and a giant package of red Twizzlers tumbled onto the counter. Jumbo bottles of pop plus the Coke quickly followed.

Snacks

"Ring 'em up, buddy," Tyrone said, like he had never seen me before. Then he tilted his head. "Hey, wait a minute. You're that new waterboy, aren't you?"

"Yeah, that's me. I'm Ed."

"And you work here at 7-Eleven?" Tyrone snickered. "Well, at least you know something about cold drinks."

"Good one, Tyrone," Fish said. "And make this fast, Waterboy. We're having a party Friday night and we have to get ready."

"Paaarteeee!" Zara wailed. She waved her forefinger and pinky in my face.

"Sounds like fun," I said, trying my best to be friendly. That was the way Bruno, the store manager, wanted us to be with customers.

Tyrone nodded. "It's going to be a blast. But don't get any ideas about going, Waterboy."

"Yeah, this party is invite only," Fish said. He pounded fists with Tyrone to let me know how exclusive the list was.

"I have to work late Friday night, anyway." Not late really, but I figured I should have a quick excuse for not being able to go.

Zara eyed me. "Maybe Ed could come by after he's finished working."

"Don't make me laugh," Tyrone said, making a face. "First, take a look at our clothes."

Tyrone, Fish and Zara nodded as they checked each other out and gave a thumbs-up. As usual, all three were dressed in the coolest shirts, jeans and kicks. I knew they spent a lot of time shopping at the mall. I didn't care much about clothes. But maybe that was because I didn't have money to spend on them in the first place.

Tyrone flicked his chin at me. "Now take a look at his 7-Eleven clothes."

"No one at our party is going to be wearing a bright green shirt with a little red seven on the chest," Fish said.

Tyrone smirked. "He looks like an ornament you'd hang on a Christmas tree."

Fish nodded. "Yeah, a tall, thin candy cane."

"Well, it was just an idea." Zara quickly met my eyes before looking away. "Ed doesn't seem so bad to me."

After packing the snacks and drinks, I pushed four heaving bags across the counter. Tyrone pulled a small black key fob out of his jeans and swung it in front of me. "Let's roll!" he said to his friends.

"To the party mobile!" Zara flashed her perfect smile.

"Hey, Waterboy, what kind of wheels do you have?" Fish asked. He struggled to pick up all the bags that Tyrone had left for him.

I knew Fish was making fun of me and started to stammer. "I don't have a —"

Snacks

"Wait, don't tell me," Fish laughed. "Your wheels are probably attached to a lame-o bike, not a car."

The three party-pals finally headed for the exit. I took a deep breath and let a long sigh hiss between my teeth. Tyrone pushed through the glass door first. Then he kept right on walking, letting it shut behind him. That left Zara to hold the door open for Fish. He was hauling all four bags like a loaded up mule. Fish lugged the packages into the parking lot and stashed them in the trunk of Tyrone's green Mustang.

Fish slammed the trunk and slid into the back seat. Zara hopped in the front beside her boyfriend. Tyrone checked himself in the rearview mirror then pressed the ignition. The powerful engine growled and I watched them pull away, as laughter flew out the open windows.

4 NO RESPECT

"Okay, listen up, everybody."

Coach Taylor clapped his thick hands together to get the attention of all the players in the locker room. Almost a head taller than Coach, I stood beside him like a skinny pencil next to a stubby eraser. "That was a big win for us against Central yesterday," he started. "But we did lose a member of our team."

The players looked up and down the benches wondering who wasn't there. "Who got hurt, Coach?" Lamar asked.

"No one got injured. But our hydration manager quit," Coach said. "Luckily we found a replacement and I want to introduce him." Coach reached up and put one of his big mitts on my bony shoulder. "This is Ed Warnicki, the new hydration manager."

"You mean waterboy, don't you, Coach?" Tyrone called from the back. The room exploded in laughter. Tyrone was the leader of the Mustangs and the rest of the team followed him like a herd of horses.

My face turned beet red. I stared up at the ceiling so I didn't have to make eye contact with any of the players.

"He looks more like the upright bar of a goalpost," joked a big linebacker named Marcus. "Any taller and we could kick a field goal between his arms."

More laughter.

"That's enough." Coach held up a hand to quiet the rowdy room. "Ed will be doing more than just filling your water bottles to keep you hydrated. He'll also be responsible for the balls. He'll make sure we have enough for practice and that they're inflated properly for the games."

"Are you sure he's strong enough to pump up the balls, Coach?" Tyrone asked as snickers rippled through the room. "I'd hate for him to suffer a pump injury and not be able fill our water bottles."

"I'm sure Ed will do just fine." Coach reached high and clapped me on the shoulder again. "He's an important part of our squad. And don't forget, without Ed you guys will be dropping like flies on the first hot day."

"That's the only thing I'll be dropping," Lamar said. The speedy receiver fist-bumped Sanjay Patel, the other wide receiver sitting beside him.

"You made two great touchdown catches, Lamar." Coach's face broke into a wide grin. "But remember the rule. Every player has to carry a water bottle throughout the school day. You have to make sure you're hydrated for practices and games. If I catch anyone without their bottle they'll run extra laps at practice. Got it?"

The players all knew Coach meant business. "Got it, Coach!"

"Now let's get out there and practise hard." Coach pointed to the door that led to the field.

The instant Coach let go of my shoulder I bolted from where the players were sitting in front of their lockers. Having thirty guys eyeballing me wasn't my idea of fun.

Over at the sink I started running cold water into the giant cooler. Then I collected the dozen water bottles and started to fill them, too. The drill was to make sure all twelve of the shared bottles were always topped off from the cooler. If a lineman squirted some water into his mouth — you filled it. If a receiver took a drink after catching a ball — you filled it. And if the quarterback threw a touchdown pass and took a few gulps — you made doubly sure you filled it. If you wanted to keep your job, that is.

After hauling the cooler out to the sideline, I set up the water table near the bench. I watched the players spread out across the field to do their stretching exercises before running some plays. It was about four o'clock on Thursday afternoon. The sun still beat down on the turf with a lot of heat.

No Respect

It wasn't long before the players began to stop by to grab drinks. After catching a few passes, Lamar came over first. "Hey, man, good to have you on the team." I waited for the joke to come, but there wasn't one. He just gave me a nod. "I know the guys gave you a rough start. Don't take it personally. Every waterboy . . . I mean . . . every hydration manager gets grilled at the beginning. The last guy couldn't take it. But just hang in there and you'll do fine."

The speedy receiver held the water bottle a few inches from his mouth and squirted. The players knew not to touch the spout with their mouths so germs didn't get spread around. Lamar handed me the bottle and sprinted back onto the field to catch more passes from Tyrone.

After a short scrimmage that pitted the Mustangs offence against the defence, Coach blew his whistle. "Let's bring it in, guys. Hit the showers."

Tyrone still held a ball as he led a bunch of the players over to the water table. "Don't guzzle down too much, boys. There'll be plenty more to drink Friday night at my party."

"And don't forget all the snacks," Marcus said as he patted his belly. "Chips are one of my favourite food groups."

"I can't wait for tomorrow." Lamar rubbed his hands together. "The whole team is showing up. Everyone here is going to be there."

"Well, not everyone." Tyrone shot me a warning glance. "You have to be a player to be invited."

"That seems a little harsh," Lamar said. "Ed might be a waterboy, but he's part of the team."

Tyrone stood his ground and shook his head. "My house, my rules."

The players took their last swigs of water and put the bottles back on the table. Then most of the team headed across the grass toward the gym door. I grabbed the big mesh bag and started to collect the footballs scattered across the field.

"Hey, Waterboy!" Tyrone yelled. "You forgot this one!" I looked up and saw a ball flying straight for me. Tyrone had fired a long pass right at my head. I wasn't sure what to do. I hadn't caught a ball in two years. With only a split second to react, I threw up my arms. *Smack!* The ball hit me square in the hands. I squeezed tight and made the catch.

"Nice snag, Waterboy," Tyrone called from the door where he stood with Lamar and Sanjay. "I didn't know you had it in you."

I stared at the football in my hands. I didn't know I had it in me, either. But I guess some things you never forget.

5 Storm AHEAD

"Hey, Ed!" Bruno shouted at me from across the store on Thursday night. He was loading some sort of orange slime into the Slurpee machine. "It's nine o'clock. Time to get outta here."

"Okay, Mr. B. See you tomorrow." When I worked on school nights I always had to rush home to do my homework. I say "rush," but my trip was never that fast. Not like it would have been in a shiny new green Mustang, for example.

I loped down the middle aisle where the Hostess Twinkies were piled up three hundred calories at a time. Then I headed out the back door to where the delivery trucks pulled up. And there it was. Leaning up against the wall just where I had left it after riding over after practice had ended — my bike.

Let me tell you about my two-wheeled steed. Instead of being made from light carbon fibre, my bag of bolts was built of heavy steel. Probably the kind that tanks and bulldozers were made from. But what do you expect from a bike you bought at a garage sale for twenty-five bucks?

Then there was my seat. I needed a freakishly high one because my legs were freakishly long. The seat post stuck up like a telephone pole. But at least it was the right height to let my stork legs stretch out.

I strapped on my silver helmet to keep whatever brains I had in one piece. Then I pulled out my phone. It had a cool app that measured how far I biked. I snapped it onto my handlebar mount. After switching on my light, I hopped on.

The sky was pitch-black and cloudy as I wheeled down the road. I had been pedalling for only a minute when I heard a sound that sent a wave of panic through me — a long, slow rumble of thunder. *Uh-oh.* At first it was just a few drops spitting on my yellow windbreaker. *No big deal*, I told myself. But then the rain started to come down in buckets. Sheets of water poured over me as if I was taking a shower. But the water wasn't soothing and warm. It was more like cold needles spiking into me. I was soaked through right away.

Raindrops pelted into my squinting eyes as I rode blindly along the shoulder of the road. Cars and trucks whizzed by. They splashed me with water from puddles that were like small lakes on the asphalt.

I swerved left and right, trying to dodge the pools of water. Drivers started honking and waving their fists at me. I yelled right back at them. But my shouts were swallowed up by the roar of their passing cars and the pounding rainstorm.

The road headed uphill and I decided to change to a lower gear. I shifted down and the pedalling got easier. Way too easy, actually. My feet started spinning frantically. I glanced down and saw my chain lying limp. It had fallen off! I stopped, grabbed the greasy chain, put it back on the sprockets and got moving again. Success. I was feeling good about the quick fix when I looked at my hands. Big gobs of black grease were smeared all over my fingers. *Could things get any worse?*

They could.

At the top of the hill, I put my head down and started to speed down the steep slope. It was a few seconds before I looked up. Sprinkled across the road ahead of me were a hundred pieces of razor-sharp glass from a broken bottle.

Pop! It was the noise no cyclist ever wants to hear — an exploding tire. I looked down. Sure enough, my rear tire had gone flat as a pancake. I stood there in the pouring rain, wondering what to do next. But I knew there was only one thing I could do. Walk. I grabbed my greasy handlebars and started to push my wounded machine forward. All around me the rain kept pelting, the cars kept splashing and the wind kept howling in my ears.

Thirty minutes later my house was in sight. I parked my bike in the garage and headed for the front door.

My shoes squished every step of the way.

I stood in the front hall. I was wetter than a drowned rat.

"You're drenched!" Mom said. She eyed the pool of water around my feet.

I took off my shirt and wrung it out, adding to the pond on the floor.

"Good thing you had a bike to get home faster," Mom said. "It would have been awful to walk."

I thought about explaining how I did have to walk. How it was the worst walk of my life. But it seemed pointless. I bit my tongue and changed the subject. "So, I've been thinking, Mom."

"Yes, dear?"

"Now that I'm working to help out, I think I need to learn how to drive."

"Well, you did just get your learner's licence." Mom smiled.

"That's the great thing about living in Alberta." I nodded. "You can start when you're only fourteen."

"And another nice thing," Mom said cheerfully, "is that we have a great car you can learn in."

I rolled my eyes. "You're kidding, right?"

Our car was a twenty-year-old Chevy. Mom called it Mildred after her sister who gave it to her. That's right. Gave it to her, for free. That should tell you something about the condition of the old beast. The colour had faded to a kind of puke-yellow and its wide body handled more like a boat than a car. That's to say it swayed wildly going around corners. I had been slammed into the passenger door more than once as Mom lurched around the streets of Calgary.

"I'll tell you what." Mom's eyebrows lifted. "Why don't I give you your first lesson?"

"Right now?" I asked, still sopping wet.

"Maybe not tonight." Mom glanced out the window at the pouring rain. "But we'll take Mildred out for a spin soon."

"Okay," I said, managing a grin. I was soaked and tired but I didn't want to give up a chance at my first driving lesson.

I mean, how bad could driving with Mom be?

6 PLAN B

"The Rams are going to be gunning for us next week."
Coach Taylor stood at midfield. He spoke to the team,
which had circled around him at the start of practice.
I stayed close by with my water bottles. I wanted to
make sure players could grab a quick drink without
having to come to the sideline.

Coach cast his gaze from player to player as he laid
out his plan for the upcoming game. "Westside is a good
team. We've got to start out fast and build a lead. That
means our passing plays have to be right on the money."
Coach pounded his meaty fist into the palm of his hand.

"We've got the best quarterback and the best receivers in the league," Tyrone said. "As long as I'm
throwing the balls, and Lamar and Sanjay are catching
them, no one can touch us. We're unbeatable."

The team started shouting and clapping their ap-
proval until Coach raised his hand. "You're right,
Tyrone. And I want to make sure it stays that way. So,
let's have the offence run some passing plays against

the defence to keep us sharp. And remember, guys, we want a healthy team next week, so no tackling today. Just cover your man."

Coach blew his whistle and the players moved into position. The defence lined up on one side of the ball. Tyrone raised his arm and called for an offensive huddle on the other. After Tyrone called a play, Lamar and Sanjay broke from the huddle and trotted to opposite sides of the field.

Taking the snap from centre, Tyrone dropped back into the pocket. He stood in the middle of the big linemen who protected him from the rushing defence. He kept his eyes on Lamar. I knew that meant the speedy wide receiver would be the target for his pass. Lamar sprinted from the line of scrimmage. He darted straight downfield before cutting to the sideline after twenty yards.

I had watched Lamar run his normal square-out route in practice over and over again. He had caught almost every pass. Lamar was Tyrone's favourite receiver and I could see why.

Tyrone pulled back his arm and fired a pass. The throw was a perfect spiral, as always. But this time the football was flying too far in front of Lamar. Lamar was fast, but not that fast. He took off like Superman and flew through the air with outstretched arms, trying to haul in the pass. Despite the superhero effort, Lamar was only able to get his fingertips on the ball. The brown leather dropped to the turf. But that wasn't the only flying object that thudded to the ground. Lamar's body plunged to the earth like a plane crashing down.

"My bad — the pass was too long!" Tyrone shouted. "Let's try it again, Lamar."

But Lamar didn't answer. He didn't even move. His body lay on the grass as still as a corpse.

By the time Coach Taylor had run to his side Lamar was writhing in pain. "It's my arm," he moaned.

Tyrone and Sanjay helped Lamar to his feet. With the injured receiver cradling his arm, the three players walked slowly to the bench where Lamar slumped down. I followed a few steps behind in case Lamar needed a cold drink. I wasn't the only one watching with concern. Zara had been taking photos on the sidelines. She rushed over after seeing the star pass catcher smash to the ground.

"Sorry, Coach." Lamar winced in pain.

"It's not your fault, Lamar." Coach kneeled down beside him. "That was a great effort."

"Maybe I'll be okay for the Westside game," Lamar groaned.

Looking at the worried faces of Coach, Tyrone and Sanjay, I could tell they didn't think Lamar would be playing next game. Or for a lot of games after that.

"You just take it easy, Lamar," Coach said. "Don't worry about the game. We'll use plan B."

Tyrone wrinkled his forehead. "Plan B, Coach?"

Coach nodded. "Sanjay becomes our number one receiver. We throw everything to him."

Plan B

"Every pass?" Tyrone threw up his hands. "The Rams are going to figure that out in a hurry, Coach. They'll double-cover Sanjay on every play. He'll never be in the clear."

Sanjay raised an eyebrow. "Who's our number two receiver, Coach?"

Coach Taylor scratched his chin. "We haven't really got one. We don't have extra players this year."

"We're going to need someone." Tyrone scanned the rest of the team. "Even if they just run straight downfield then stop and turn around. There must be someone who can do that and catch the ball."

"Water, anyone?" I asked, holding out a bottle.

Sanjay took a sip and tossed the bottle back to me. I caught it in one hand.

Sanjay locked eyes with me. "Hey, Ed, you can catch."

"It's just a water bottle," I said. "It's no big deal."

"Yeah, but I've seen you catch a football, too," Sanjay said. "At the end of yesterday's practice when Tyrone threw the ball at you."

"Is that true, Warnicki?" Coach asked. "Did you catch a pass from Tyrone?"

"Just a fluke, Coach." I shrugged.

Sanjay's eyes widened. "What do you think about Ed being our number two receiver, Coach?"

"I don't know," Coach said, giving me the once-over. "He's way too tall and way too skinny. He's not what I would call football material. I don't want someone else getting hurt." He raised an eyebrow. "What do you think, Ed? Does being a receiver for the Mustangs sound good?"

I didn't know if I could catch the passes or not. But playing for the Mustangs was something I had always dreamed about. "Maybe, Coach." I shrugged again.

"I know we're desperate, but Waterboy is no receiver," Tyrone scoffed. "You just have to look at him to see that."

"You're right," Coach said as he flipped the ball to Tyrone. "Let's try a pass play and really see what kind of receiver Ed is."

Tyrone shrugged and looked me straight in the eye. "Okay, Waterboy, I want you to use those giraffe legs and run as fast as you can downfield for twenty yards then curl around and catch the ball."

"Wear this," Sanjay said, handing me his helmet. "That will make it seem more like a game."

"And protect you if you fall over yourself," Tyrone said. "Which you probably will."

I strapped on the green helmet and got ready to run. Tyrone called out the signals for a pass play, "Red . . . 32 . . . hut . . . hut!" He nodded at me after the second *hut* and I took off down the field. I ran as fast as I could. My skinny arms pumped beside me and my long legs loped beneath me. Twenty steps later I stopped and turned around. The ball was right there just like Tyrone said it would be. All I had to do was hold out my hands and the ball would land in them. I'd make the catch and everyone would be impressed. But I froze. This wasn't the park with my dad, and I wasn't twelve years old. This was a real football field, with a coach, a whole team and a reporter watching me.

The ball hit my hands and fell to the ground. I hung my head.

"Good try, Ed!" Coach shouted. "You almost had it. Just squeeze the ball a little harder next time."

Tyrone looked puzzled. "Next time, Coach?"

"Just like you said, we're desperate." Coach patted Tyrone's shoulder pads. "Besides, have you got a better plan?"

Tyrone let out a long sigh. Then he shook his head and glanced at Lamar slumped on the bench. "We're going to miss you, man." Tyrone headed to the sideline for a drink.

From the corner of my eye I watched Zara move in to interview the Mustangs quarterback. She started by asking Tyrone what every Mustangs fan wanted to know. "Now that Lamar is hurt and you're down to only one good receiver, what's your prediction for the Westside game next week?"

"We have no chance," Tyrone said, shooting me a nasty look. "No chance at all."

7 Second CHANCE

Coach Taylor blew his whistle and told everyone to take a timeout from the practice. I still felt bad about dropping the pass a few minutes before.

"Take a break, Ed," Coach said. "We'll give it another shot later."

I trudged over to the bench and slumped down beside Lamar. He was waiting for an assistant coach to take him to the hospital to get his arm checked out.

"Hey, Ed, you look in worse shape than I do." Lamar managed a weak smile.

"I'm no receiver," I said, shaking my head. "If I can't catch a perfect pass like that, I can't catch anything. I don't blame Tyrone for thinking I'm useless. I might as well give up."

Lamar gave me a sideways glance. "You may not be built like most receivers, Ed." He looked down at my long legs sticking out in front of the bench. Then up at my spindly arms. "But I know you can catch, man."

"How do you know that?"

"I saw you pull in the pass that Tyrone threw at your head last practice. That was a great catch, dude. You had lightning-fast reflexes. If that had been in a game, the fans would have been on their feet. You just have to believe you can catch the ball."

"I don't know. I haven't played football in a long time. And when I did play it was with my dad. But he's not coming back . . . ever."

Lamar nodded. "I hear you, man. My dad left a few years ago, too. It's tough."

Coach waved at me from the middle of the field. "Okay, Ed, let's give this another try."

Lamar gave me a serious nod. "You can do it, Ed."

I wasn't so sure I could do it. Wishing I had Lamar's faith in me, I walked over to where Coach was waiting with Tyrone and Sanjay.

"Okay, Ed, we're going to ask you to run a couple of pass routes," Coach said. "First, let's try a post."

I looked at Coach, puzzled. When I played with Dad, I just ran and caught the ball. I didn't know what different routes were called.

"Sanjay will show you," Coach said.

Tyrone snapped the ball to himself and Sanjay bolted. He ran straight down the side of the field then cut toward the goalpost in the middle. Tyrone threw the ball and Sanjay caught it while running at top speed. He made it look easy.

Long Bomb

Sanjay ran back and tossed the ball to Tyrone. "See, nothing to it," the quarterback said.

"Okay, Ed, your turn." Coach clapped his hands together.

Tyrone snapped the pigskin and I took off. My legs were so long it took me a while to get up to full speed. After about ten yards I ran toward the goalpost in the middle of the field. I was so busy keeping my eye on the goalpost I forgot to do one thing — turn around and catch the pass.

Thud!

The football hit me square in the back.

"What are you doing, Waterboy!" Tyrone shouted. "You have to watch for the pass!" He shot a look at Coach. "This is hopeless. We just have one receiver and that's Sanjay. I've been throwing passes to Sanjay for years. I know him and he knows me. I trust him to catch the ball. I don't trust Waterboy to catch anything but a bottle. We're still going to get killed in that game against Westside."

I trotted back to Coach, Tyrone and Sanjay. "Sorry," I said. "I forgot to turn around."

Tyrone shook his head. "No kidding."

I handed Sanjay's helmet back to him. "I guess I'll go back to being the waterboy."

"Not yet," Coach said. "We need you, Ed. Tyrone, crank out one more to Stretch."

"If you say so, Coach." Tyrone nodded. "But we're wasting our time."

This time I was ready.

"Ready, hut, go!" Tyrone shouted as he snapped the ball to himself.

I sprinted from the line, again. My long strides were slow at first, again. I angled toward the goalpost, again. But this time I looked back. Tyrone's throw was already in the air coming straight for me. I put out my hands and grabbed the ball. Then I galloped into the end zone.

I almost couldn't believe I had caught the pass. I ran back to the group with the ball in my hands and a small smile on my face.

"Nice snag, Ed," Coach said.

"Now we've got two receivers." Sanjay smiled.

"I'm not so sure." Tyrone crossed his arms. "Anyone could have caught that pass. There was no one even covering Waterboy. Playing in a game is a lot different."

Coach blew his whistle. "Okay, guys, that's it for today. Hit the showers."

A big crowd of players joined Tyrone before heading off the field. "Don't forget the party at my place tonight, boys," he said. "And remember, it's for players only."

"What about Ed?" Lamar asked. "Now that he's on the team, he's invited, right?"

Looking me straight in the eyes, Tyrone shook his head. "He hasn't proven himself in a bunch of games yet. He's still just the waterboy to me."

Long Bomb

Tyrone was right. Even though I'd be wearing a Mustangs uniform next game, someone still had to clean up the field. That someone was me. I started to pick up the water bottles and balls.

As Tyrone walked to the sideline, Zara swooped in for another interview. "Looks like Ed the waterboy is going to take Lamar's place. What do you think about our chances against Westside now?" Zara held up her phone to record Tyrone's answer.

"No one can replace Lamar. He's the best. As far as Ed the waterboy is concerned, he's the worst. So, our chances still don't look good."

8 MILDRED

It was Friday night. While the rest of the team was at Tyrone's party, I was at work selling Big Gulps. At the end of my shift I said goodbye to Bruno and rode home on my patched-up bike. At least the sky wasn't raining and my tires weren't popping like the night before.

I put my bike away and trudged through the front door.

"So, are you ready, Ed?" My mom was waiting for me.

"For what, Mom?"

"Your first driving lesson in Mildred."

"I'm beat after football practice and working. I was just going to chill tonight."

Mom jangled the car keys in her hand. "You need a break from all that work, Ed. Besides, I thought you wanted to learn right away."

"I do, but I'm still saving up for Driver Education classes. They're hundreds of dollars."

Mom raised an eyebrow. "You could wait until

then. Or you could get behind the wheel with me right now."

I couldn't argue with that. Maybe getting a taste of the road before my classes was a good idea. "Okay, let's go."

Mildred was waiting for us in the garage. The driver's seat was pushed so far forward for Mom that I couldn't even climb into the car. I pushed it all the way back and slid in. Then I turned the key and the engine sputtered to life. Reaching down to the gearshift, I put the old beast in reverse and slowly backed out of the garage.

"Wait!" Mom shrieked.

I hit the brakes and the puke-yellow car jerked to a stop. We hadn't even got halfway down the driveway.

"Did you check the sidewalk for children walking or skateboarding or biking?" Words fired out of Mom's mouth like bullets from a machine gun. "Did you check the street for passing cars?"

"How many little kids are going to be out at this time of night, Mom?"

"Driving rule number one," Mom said, sternly. "You can never be too careful."

I let out a long sigh and looked left and right. No kids. No cars. I backed out onto the street and started to drive away. I was feeling pretty good when another howl came from the passenger seat.

"Do you see that stop sign?"

I nodded. "You mean the one that's way down at the end of the street?"

"Yes, that one." Mom thrust her head forward. She stared through the windshield as if she was looking through binoculars on a secret spy mission. "Rule number two — it's never too early to slow down."

I rolled to a halt in front of the red sign, then stepped on the gas.

"Did you come to a complete stop?" Mom burst out. "I think we were still moving. Did you look both ways? I'm not sure you did." Mom's head swivelled left and right like an owl searching for prey.

Driving at a snail's pace, we continued to crawl along. It would have been faster to walk. But I couldn't complain — at least I was on the road.

Knowing Tyrone lived in the rich part of the neighbourhood, I made the next left and turned onto his street. I may not have been invited to his party but there was no law against me driving by his house. The closer we got, the more parked cars lined the street. *Tyrone wasn't kidding about this being a monster party*, I thought. I could hear the music pounding from the speakers two blocks away.

Mom wasn't impressed. "I don't think the neighbours want to hear all that racket." She cracked the window an inch and the throbbing bass filled the car. *Boom . . . boom . . . boom.* Mom winced as she covered her ears and quickly closed the window again.

As we crept along the street, I watched three shadowy figures leave the front door of the huge party house.

"Stop the car, Ed!" Mom wailed.

Long Bomb

Was there something on the road? A dog . . . a cat . . . a crazed squirrel? I hammered the brakes and the car lurched to a halt at the end of Tyrone's driveway. It was none of those things. I twisted my head to see Mom reaching for the door handle. *You're not doing what I think you're doing, are you?* I prayed silently. Mom stepped out of the car and huffed her way toward the three figures now standing under the streetlights. It was Tyrone, Fish and Zara!

This can't be happening! I thought. I tried to slouch down in my seat. But when your legs are as long as hockey sticks, this is a tricky move. They bumped the dash and I groaned.

"Excuse me," Mom said to the biggest of the three. "Do you know who lives here?"

Tyrone nodded. "I do."

"Then you should turn down the music." Mom wagged a disapproving finger at the star quarterback and most popular guy at Calgary High. "You're bothering all the neighbours."

Tyrone started to smile but he wasn't grinning at Mom. He walked right past her up to the side of Mildred and knocked on the window. "Is that you in there, Waterboy?"

I gave a feeble nod and lowered my window.

Tyrone stood back and eyeballed the old car that was taking up half the road. "Sweet ride, Eddy."

"Yeah, nice wheels," Fish laughed. "But last century called and they want their car back."

Zara rubbed her chin. She seemed perplexed by

the vehicle in front of her. "I've never seen a car that colour yellow before, Ed. What is it — creamed corn or hotdog mustard?"

I turned off the car and the engine clunked and shuddered to a stop. This had been a big mistake. An epic fail. I never should have driven down this street. What was I thinking?

Leaning out the window, I whisper-shouted as loud as I could. "Mom, get back in the car — let's go!"

Mom was riled up and in no hurry to leave. She gave Tyrone one more finger wag and said, "Do your parents know what you're up to, young man?"

"They sure do." Tyrone's grin grew wider. "In fact, they're inside at the party. Probably cranking the tunes and dancing right now. Do you want to come in and join them, Mrs. Warnicki? I bet you could really bust a move."

"Mom!" I pleaded. "I'm begging you. Get in the car."

After the longest thirty seconds of my life, Mom finally marched back to the passenger side and got in. Her face was flushed and her head was shaking so fast it was almost vibrating. "Take me home, Ed. There's no reasoning with the young people of today. This driving lesson is over."

She didn't have to ask me twice. I turned the key and put my foot on the gas pedal, and we made our escape. With my heart still thumping, I glanced in the rearview mirror. Tyrone, Zara and Fish were doubled over laughing as we drove away.

9 Clowning AROUND

I slammed my textbook shut.

Math was over. The whiteboard was a mess of equations and formulas. Unfortunately, I only understood about half of them. I should have been paying more attention, but my mind was on the game coming up. Math was Monday's last class and I bolted out the door. Racing back to my locker, I passed one of the huge football posters hanging in the hallway. Giant green letters were painted above a green football helmet with a white Mustang on its side. The headline was a warning for our archrivals the Westside Rams: *DANGER: STAMPEDE COMING!*

"Hey, Waterboy!" a whiny voice shouted behind me. "Shouldn't you be on your way to the locker room? We have a big game you know."

I spun around to see Fish and Zara fast approaching.

"Let's go," Zara said. She was almost pulling Fish down the hall. "I'm reporting on the game and I'm late."

As they rushed by, Zara looked over her shoulder at me. "Maybe I'll see you on the sidelines, Ed."

Did Zara just say she'd see me at the game? I wondered. *Was she smiling when she said it? What did she mean by that?*

I hopped down the stairs two at a time. Then I snaked through the crowded hallway, dodging a parade of kids who only came up to my shoulders. Flying into the gym, I rushed toward the locker room and pushed through the door. Every head turned to watch my entrance.

"That was close," Tyrone said, pretending to be serious. "We almost had to play the game without our new receiver, Waterboy."

Most of the players snickered, then went back to putting on their equipment.

"Better put on your gear, Ed," Lamar said. He was standing in front of his locker with a sling around his neck. "You don't want to be late."

My eyes widened. "But I don't have any gear! Last week I was just the waterboy and didn't need any equipment."

"I'd lend you mine but I don't think it would fit." Lamar walked over and stood next to me. He was so much shorter that I could've rested my arm on his shoulder.

Coach Taylor came over, looking concerned. "You can't play in your school clothes, Ed." Then his face turned into a smile. "There should be some extra gear in the storage room."

I ran next door and flicked on the light. The room smelled like stinky old sweat. There were a couple of big cardboard boxes marked *Mustangs* on the side. I ripped open the first one. There were a few pads lying in the bottom. It was equipment that no one else wanted. I pulled out some pants, shoulder pads and a green Mustangs jersey. In the second box I found a helmet and a pair of old black cleats. Would all this gear fit me? I had my doubts but I had no choice. The opening kick-off was only a few minutes away. I pulled on the leftover gear and rushed back to join the rest of the team.

The locker room fell silent. Everyone was staring at me.

"You look like a green scarecrow," Tyrone said, gawking at my uniform.

Sanjay pointed out, "Your helmet is too big, your jersey is too small and your pants are too short."

Lamar shrugged. "Ed doesn't look that bad, does he?"

"Are you kidding?" Tyrone said. "Did the circus just pull into town? Waterboy's cleats are so long they look like clown shoes." Tyrone broke out laughing at the old cleats that were a few sizes too big.

I felt like a geek knowing my uniform didn't fit. How could it? I had to make do with leftover gear that was too big or too small for everyone else. I wasn't built like any of the other players. I might have been the youngest guy on the team, but I was also the tallest. I found a locker in the far corner and sat down, hoping no one would notice me.

Coach Taylor put two fingers in his mouth and whistled to get everyone's attention. Not that he had to — everyone was waiting for him to give his pre-game pep talk. "Westside is a good team, sometimes a great team. We have to be prepared right from the opening kick-off. We can't let them get ahead. We don't want to play catch-up football. That means our defence has to be ready. Are you ready, defence?"

"Yes, Coach!"

"And it means our offence has to be set right from the first play from scrimmage. We have to mix our running and passing plays so the Rams won't know what's coming next. Are you ready, offence?"

"Yes, Coach!"

Tyrone leaped to his feet. "Let's do this, Mustangs!"

The star quarterback raised his right arm and led the team to the door. A line of green uniforms charged behind him. All the players were shouting. I stayed back. I didn't know if I had the courage to go out and play. I took a deep breath and walked through the door.

10 Action JACKSON

The Mustangs ran onto the field and were hit by a wall of sound.

A large crowd was already cheering in the stands. On one side of the field were our fans from Calgary High. The Mustangs cheerleaders were performing their dance routines in front of the bleachers. Our students sang along.

We're the best, we can't be beat.

Mustangs will never taste defeat!

Busloads of students from Westside were in the stands on the other side of the field. This seemed like a smart move. I'd hate to think what would happen if the two crowds got too close to each other. There was no love lost between our schools. The Mustangs and Rams were both powerhouse squads. Some years Westside won the football championship and some years we did. Sure, there were other teams in the league. But they never posed much of a threat.

I paced nervously on the sideline, waiting for the

Mustangs to receive the opening kick-off. In another minute I'd be playing in my first game. My heart pounded. The kick was in the air and Levi caught the ball. He ran it back to our fifty-yard line before being tackled. It was an awesome return.

"Let's go, offence!" Coach Taylor shouted.

I strapped on my helmet and followed Tyrone onto the field. The Calgary fans were screaming at the top of their lungs:

Jackson, Jackson he's our man!
If he can't do it, nobody can!

We huddled around our quarterback. Tyrone's eyes flashed from player to player. But he skipped over me and went right to our number-one receiver. "Hook to Sanjay on three," Tyrone called out. I was glad the pass was to Sanjay and not me. I hadn't learned all the pass routes yet. And I wasn't sure I could catch one anyway. Lining up far to the right side, I watched the play.

Tyrone stood over our centre and called for the ball. "Hut . . . hut . . . hut!" On the third *hut*, Tyrone grabbed the pigskin and raced back into the pocket. The Westside front four tried to rush but they were no match for our linemen. The beefy players were like a brick wall. Tyrone watched Sanjay run down the field then fired the pass. After ten yards, Sanjay hooked around and looked back for the pass. The ball was right on the money. All Sanjay had to do was grab it.

"First down!" the referee shouted.

Long Bomb

Tyrone then called a running play. He handed off the ball to our fullback. Levi bulldozed his way up the middle for a big gain. The big quarterback was leading our Mustangs offence down the field. Tyrone was like a magician. One play he'd call a pass to Sanjay. Then he'd hand the ball to Levi or Carlos for a running play. The Westside defence never knew what to expect from our number twelve.

As I watched Tyrone, I wondered how he did it. How he was so confident. How he knew every pass would be caught. How every run would be for a first down. I never knew how things would turn out. Whether I'd catch a pass or drop it. Or whether I'd ever stop growing.

Two plays later we were in the red zone — only twenty yards to go for a touchdown.

"Corner to Sanjay," Tyrone barked out in the huddle. "Make sure you get in the clear."

On the next play Tyrone dropped back in the pocket to pass. He found Sanjay open in the corner of the end zone for the score. The speedy receiver snagged the perfect pass and spiked the ball into the ground to celebrate. Touchdown!

A wave of Mustangs fans jumped to their feet and cheered wildly. It was easy to see why Tyrone was so popular, at least with the Calgary students. For the Westside students across the field, not so much.

I could hear the boos from the Rams supporters.

They had to watch Tyrone and Sanjay being mobbed by our Mustangs teammates. Then Tyrone broke from the group and ran in front of the Westside fans seated in the bleachers. He held up a single finger to show which team was number one. He was just rubbing it in, and the Westside students started to get angry. Their jeers got louder.

"Hey, number twelve," shouted a Rams fan in the first row. "You suck!"

After taunting the Westside students, Tyrone ran back toward us. I high-fived Sanjay and ran off the field with the rest of the offence. I may not have touched the ball, but at least I had been on the field when we scored.

Grabbing a water bottle, I noticed Zara standing beside the Mustangs bench. I stared for a few seconds, hoping she'd look back at me. But she was too busy scribbling in her notebook. Every so often she would put away her pen and snap a few game photos with the camera that hung around her neck. She looked like a real pro reporter.

After our defence stopped the Rams, our offence was back on the field. On the first play, Tyrone fired a pass to Sanjay as he streaked down the sideline. The Mustangs new number-one receiver hauled the ball in and raced another twenty-five yards into the Rams end zone. Another touchdown for Sanjay!

The team was on a roll. By the time the fourth

quarter came around, the Mustangs were up by three touchdowns. We had a lock on the win.

Standing on the sideline, I could hear Coach Taylor talking. "Great job, Tyrone," he said. "Sanjay has had a big game, but he's looking a little tired. This would be a good time to give Ed a chance."

My heart jumped when I heard my name. But it was clear Tyrone wasn't thrilled with the idea. "If you say so, Coach. But only because we're way out front."

I jogged onto the field with the Mustangs offence and huddled up. Tyrone scanned the players and stopped at me. "Okay, Waterboy, this is your chance. Button hook on two."

I stared at him blankly. *What's a button hook?*

"Take five steps forward and turn around, bro." Tyrone shook his head at me.

I lined up across from the Rams defensive back. He was hardly paying any attention to me. Why would he? A pass hadn't come close to me all afternoon. The ball was snapped on Tyrone's second *hut* and I ran from the line of scrimmage. I took five long strides and hooked around. No one was covering me. I was in the clear. Looking up, I saw the football flying toward me. I had to catch it. I had to prove to Tyrone and Coach that I could do it. My arms reached out, but the ball flew right through my hands and hit me hard in the chest. I thought it was going to bounce away. I thought I was going drop it. But I held the ball against my body and fell to the ground.

Action Jackson

"Nice grab," Sanjay said as we ran back to the huddle. "It was only five yards, but you caught it, man."

Tyrone wasn't buying it. "You got lucky, Waterboy. But don't expect me to pass to you again."

I was looking at Tyrone but I wasn't really listening. I was still thinking about my first catch in a game. It made me feel like I was part of the team. The only problem was that a lot of players didn't think I should be on the squad — including our quarterback.

11 The DISCOVERY

I stood on the sidelines watching the clock tick down. The game against the Rams was almost over. It felt good to be on the winning side. It felt even better that I had made a catch and helped the team. Even if it was just a short pass.

The Calgary fans had started to count down the last seconds: "Three . . . two . . . one . . . yeah!" The stands exploded into a cheering frenzy. A wave of fist pumping and hand clapping spread through the Mustangs crowd. The referee blew the final whistle. I checked the scoreboard: Calgary 35, Westside 14.

The Mustangs fans emptied out of the bleachers. They raced onto the field to celebrate the big win, but they weren't alone. A group of Rams supporters on the other side of the field dashed onto the turf as well. These fans weren't looking to join the party. They were looking for trouble. And they found it.

As usual, Fish was in the middle of all the pushing and shoving. But he was just mouthing off. He was good at starting fights, not finishing them. "You want a piece of me?" Fish taunted a couple of guys wearing blue Westside jackets. "You'll have to catch me first." The two hefty Westside students tried to chase down Fish. But the small pest zigzagged between them and escaped their clutches.

It took a few teachers from both schools to break up the scuffles that had broken out. Finally, the Westside students headed back to the buses, shaking their fists at the Calgary fans. They were still mad about the loss.

Back at our Mustangs bench, Zara was busy getting quotes from the star quarterback. Tyrone had taken off his helmet and made sure his hair was just right. He was all smiles. A small group of Calgary fans were huddled around Tyrone and Zara, listening to the interview.

"Great game, Tyrone!" Zara beamed as she held up her phone to record the conversation.

"Never in doubt." Tyrone smiled right back at her. "We had them right from the first play."

"Do you think Westside could ever steal a win from Calgary?" Zara pushed her phone a little closer to the quarterback's mouth.

Tyrone scoffed before answering. "The Rams couldn't steal a win if we handed it to them."

The small crowd of Calgary fans laughed along with Tyrone.

Zara snapped a few photos of Tyrone pretending

to make a pass before packing up. Then she pocketed her phone.

"Interview over already?" Tyrone asked. "I've got lots more to say."

"I'm sure you do." Zara grinned. "But I've got to write up the story. It was a big win and the Calgary fans want to read all about it in the *Mustang News*." She gave a quick wave. "Later, gator."

Inside the locker room, the players were whooping it up. Everyone was shouting, high-fiving and fist-bumping each other. Everyone except me, that is. Most of the players just walked by as if I wasn't there. Sanjay high-fived me, but then quickly joined the rest of the team. He called me over. I took one look at my gear and knew I didn't fit in. I pulled off my equipment right away so it wouldn't remind my teammates how geeky I looked.

After a quick shower I got dressed in my school clothes. They didn't fit me that well, either. My shirt was too baggy for my skinny chest. And my jeans were too short for my long, bony legs. But at least I didn't look like a scarecrow or a clown.

There was no point hanging around. After picking up my bike helmet, I started toward the door. I didn't say goodbye to anyone because I didn't want to draw attention to myself. No such luck.

"Hey, Waterboy," Tyrone shouted from his locker. "Pedalling your tricycle home?" I nodded glumly and kept walking. "Too bad you don't have some real wheels."

I trudged out of the school and headed across the parking lot to get my bike from the racks.

"Wait up, Ed!"

I recognized the voice right away. Whirling my head around, I saw Zara running to catch up. I was so tongue-tied all I could do was give her a goofy grin. "Great interview," I croaked.

"Just doing my job," Zara said, a little out of breath. "Tyrone makes it easy. He's some kind of quarterback."

Even I had to admit he was pretty good. "Yeah, he's all right."

We walked in awkward silence for a few more steps until we got to Tyrone's car. The green muscle machine looked fast even when it was parked. I knew Zara was impressed and I wanted to ignore the car. But then something caught my eye and my jaw dropped. "Look at that!"

"What the —" Zara shrieked, pointing at the side of the car. "Who would do a thing like that?" Zara's reporter skills kicked in and she started taking photos. "Tyrone is going to lose his mind when he sees this."

I couldn't stop staring at the shiny Mustang. Someone had spray-painted graffiti on the side of the car. The words *Rams Rule!* were scrawled across the green door in big black letters.

Long Bomb

Zara's eyes were wild with shock. "It must have just happened!"

I moved in for a closer look and nodded. "The paint is still dripping down the side."

My eyes darted left and right. I checked to see if anyone was running away. If there were any suspects. But the parking lot was empty.

12 BLOW UP

The next day, the cafeteria was packed.

I sat by myself and picked through a half-eaten carton of fries. Every so often I'd wipe a smear of red ketchup from my lips. *Maybe Mom has a point about me being a messy eater*, I thought. At the next table, Tyrone, Fish and Sanjay sat with a few other players, wolfing down their lunches. There were trays full of burgers, hot dogs and slices of pizza. Even though I sat close by, I don't think they even noticed I was there. It was just like in the locker room.

"Did you read about yesterday's game in the *Mustang News*?" Sanjay asked. He held up his phone to show the online story.

"Great shot of our man Tyrone." Fish pointed at Zara's photo of Tyrone with one hand while slapping his hero on the back with the other.

"And how about Tyrone's quote?" Sanjay said. "That's really going to get under the skin of those guys over at Westside."

Long Bomb

Fish reached out and bumped fists with the star quarterback. "You saying the Rams couldn't steal a win even if we handed it to them, was classic Tyrone, Tyrone."

Tyrone nodded. "Zara really knows how to write a story that gets a reaction."

"She sure does," a girl's voice cut in.

I turned to see Zara weaving her way through the long tables to where the players sat.

Tyrone's face lit up. "Hey, where did you come from, Zara?"

"Just passing through the caf." Zara knifed her palm through the air like a shark swimming through water. "On my way to the *Mustang News* office. Going to write a preview of the team's big rematch against the Rams."

"Make sure you mention my name." Tyrone gave Zara his million-dollar smile.

"What about the rest of us?" a beefy lineman kidded. He knew there was little hope of Zara writing about the big front four instead of their talented quarterback.

Suddenly, the jokey conversation turned serious. Sanjay looked up wide-eyed from reading his phone. "You should see what's happening on social. The Rams have got hold of the story and they're bent out of shape. Snapchat is blowing up, man!"

Phones lit up all around the table. No one was allowed to have a phone in a classroom, but the cafeteria was different. Lunchtime was the only chance to check messages and social.

"So is Instagram!" Tyrone said.

"Plus Facebook and Twitter!" Fish added, eyes bulging out of his head.

"They must have hacked into the Calgary High website." Zara's dark eyes flashed around the table. "That's the only place you can read the story."

I grabbed my phone and scrolled through my Twitter feed. Players and students from Westside were posting all over it.

@WestsideGang: You may have robbed the first game @Mustangs but we're going to steal the second. #RamsRule!

That was bad but it got worse. There was a photo under the next tweet.

@WestsideGang: It's payback time @Mustangs. #RamsRule!

I thumbed down and there it was — Tyrone's green Mustang with the black graffiti sprayed on the side. Whoever painted the car had also taken a picture of it.

A few seconds later Fish found the photo, too. "Hey, guys, check out hashtag Rams Rule."

Tyrone and the other Mustangs players quickly tracked down the hashtag and the posting.

"I can't believe it!" Sanjay's eyes were glued to his screen. "What happened to your car, man?"

"No big deal," Tyrone said, laughing it off. "Just some Westside fans unhappy after the game. Must have been that last touchdown pass I threw to you." Tyrone reached out and bumped fists with Sanjay.

"Those fans were a lot more than unhappy." Zara gave Tyrone a worried look. "Ed and I couldn't believe what they had written on your car."

Tyrone narrowed his eyes at Zara. "Ed? You didn't tell me you were with Waterboy in the parking lot after the game."

"You never asked." Zara shrugged.

When I heard my name I swallowed hard. *This might be a good time to find another seat*, I told myself. I picked up my fries and moved a couple of tables over. I was far enough away to keep out of Tyrone's way, but close enough to hear them talk.

Fish shook his head at the photo of the car. "That's low even for them. Those Westside jerks will do anything to throw Tyrone off his game."

"You can relax," Tyrone assured him. "Because it's not going to work. I called the cops and they're looking into it. Plus, I've already had the car repainted at my dad's dealership." Tyrone tapped another message on his phone. "There, that should take care of these Westside clowns."

I checked my Twitter feed and saw Tyrone's message posted along with a photo of his newly painted car door.

Blow Up

@QBTyrone: Like it never happened
#RamsFool! #RamsRule!

Fish pounded fists with Tyrone again. "That'll show 'em. Nothing rattles our man Tyrone."

"I've got a deadline," Zara said. She flicked her head toward the exit. "Catch you later."

Tyrone swallowed his last bite of pizza and pulled a final sip from his straw. Then he stood up to join her. "Meet you dudes at practice after school."

Seeing his two friends about to leave, Fish jumped up as well. "Yeah, dudes, we have to split."

Tyrone and Zara snaked through the maze of cafeteria tables. Fish tailed them a few steps behind. I dabbed a fry in some ketchup and checked the thread of postings on my phone. The last one was a mystery. I scratched my head and wondered what it meant.

@WestsideGang: There's more to steal than a game. #RamsRule!

13 Heavy WEIGHT

Clang!

After practice we hit the gym. There were some strong dudes on our team. Hefty linemen, muscled running backs and wiry cornerbacks worked out all the time. The only exercise I got was riding my bike. I grabbed my water bottle and stepped into the weight room.

The place was noisy. Music was thumping out of overhead speakers. Guys were groaning, trying to pump as much iron as they could. A lot of iron was hitting the ground when the weights were put down.

Clang . . . clang . . . clang!

It was my first time in the weight room. I had never even lifted a barbell before. As I glanced at myself in the mirror on the wall, I could see that was pretty clear. I looked like a broom handle when I turned sideways. The other guys on the team sure weren't built like me. They were all jacked.

In the far corner a few players had gathered around the bench press. One was lying on his back on the padded bench. His arms were pushing up a metal bar over his chest. Heavy black weights hung on both ends. With a crowd of players in my way, I couldn't see who it was. But he must have been strong. I figured it was one of our big linemen.

"I've never seen someone push so much weight," Sanjay said. He shook his head in disbelief. "I couldn't lift half as much."

"That must be a team record," Levi said, amazed.

I took a few steps closer. My eyes popped. It was Tyrone.

"One!" counted the group of players. Tyrone pushed up the bar and let it back down.

"Two!" the players said a little louder as he pushed the iron again.

"Three!" This time the players cheered as Tyrone did his third and last push.

The group of players watching split up. They grabbed their water bottles and went back to lifting their own weights under Coach Taylor's watchful eye. I stayed put, still stunned by Tyrone's strength.

"What are you looking at, Waterboy?" Tyrone narrowed his eyes at me as he sat up on the bench.

"I didn't know how strong you were." I couldn't stop staring at Tyrone's ripped muscles.

Tyrone looked me up and down. I was wearing green shorts and a white T-shirt just like everyone else. "And I didn't know how weak you were."

I glanced down at my bony arms and legs. "Maybe I should try doing what you just did."

Tyrone smirked. "No one can do what I just did, bro. Check out these guns." Tyrone held up both arms and admired his bulging biceps. Then he shot me a look. "You know Zara likes her men strong, not scrawny."

I didn't know if that's what Zara really did like. But I figured getting stronger couldn't hurt, just in case.

Tyrone pointed at my stick arms. "You could use a weight-lifting coach, Waterboy. And I know just who that should be."

I raised an eyebrow. "Who?"

This time Tyrone smiled. "Me, bro."

Pumping iron was something I knew I should do. But I wasn't so sure Tyrone should be the one coaching me.

"Slide under the bar, Waterboy," Tyrone ordered. "Let's see what you've got."

I lay on the bench and put my hands on the bar above my chest.

"Okay, show me what you're made of," Tyrone said.

I pushed as hard as I could. The bar didn't even budge.

"I didn't think so, Waterboy." Tyrone pulled off some weights from the end of the bar. "Try again. Even Zara could lift this puny amount."

Heavy Weight

I pushed. I grunted. I groaned. My face turned red. The bar still didn't move.

Tyrone sighed. "Do you even have muscles, Waterboy?" He pulled off almost all the weights and put them on the floor.

By now a small crowd had come over to watch. I wanted to forget the whole thing and leave. But a ring of players had me boxed in. I gritted my teeth and pushed again. This time the bar moved. An inch at first. Then a bit more. Finally, my arms were straight up. I eased the bar down and let out a long breath. I was beat from doing just one rep.

"Nice work," Tyrone scoffed. "You're now officially the weakest guy on the team."

I slid out from under the bar and went to sit on a bench against the wall. I took a swig from my water bottle. Lamar sat down beside me. He had been watching the whole thing. "Don't worry about it, Ed," he said. "A pass receiver doesn't have to be the strongest guy on the team. He just has to have the best hands." Lamar watched me hold out my long fingers. "And you got that, bro."

I had never thought that having long fingers was an advantage. They just seemed to get in the way. But they did wrap around the ball when I tried to catch it. I just had to be in the right position to catch it. I had to know my pass routes.

But strength was a whole different story. "It's easy for you to say being strong isn't important," I replied.

Even though Lamar's arm was in a sling, his muscles bulged under his T-shirt. "You're almost as strong as Tyrone. I'm sure you were never built like me." I waved my toothpick arms in the air.

"I have to admit you are pretty skinny, Ed," Lamar chuckled. "But I wasn't much bigger when I started."

Both my eyebrows shot up. "I don't believe you."

"It's true." Lamar nodded. "But I worked at it and built myself up a little bit at a time. You can't expect to get stronger overnight."

I let out a small laugh. "I think it would take me years."

"There's only one way to find out, you know."

Getting stronger would take a lot of work and a lot of time. I knew that. But I was sick of Tyrone and the other players making fun of me. If I wanted to be a better receiver I had to get stronger. I had to be able to run faster and jump higher to catch the ball. I had to be able to get tackled without getting snapped in half. And if Lamar was willing to help me, I couldn't say no.

"When do we start, Lamar?"

"How about right now?"

14 Special DELIVERY

That night was a slow one. Only a few customers had come into the 7-Eleven. They were mostly parents stopping on their way home from work to pick up milk or bread. Then the door swung open and Zara walked in. I waited for Tyrone and Fish to follow, but they were nowhere to be seen. Zara was there by herself.

I gulped.

I watched her bop down the aisle to the back of the store. Her spiky black hair was just visible over the top row of shelves. She tucked the book she was carrying under her arm and reached into the cooler case. I had asked Bruno to put the Cokes on a lower level so they were in easy reach for her to grab. Zara turned and walked straight back toward me. She placed the bottle and book on the counter to dig in her bag for money. I glanced down and saw the book was the driver education handbook. *Zara must be learning how to drive too*, I thought.

I needed a joke, a wisecrack, a funny story to get the conversation going. "Is your driver handbook *yielding* any tips?" I asked.

Zara stared up at me blankly. "What? Oh, I get it — *yielding* like a yield sign. Very clever, Ed."

Strike one. Zara didn't seem amused by my first attempt at humour. I turned my attention to the bottle of Coke. "Picking up dinner?" It was an equally lame line.

Zara looked serious. "I know pop isn't healthy, but I need to keep up my energy tonight."

Strike two. Not wanting to strike out, I quit trying to be a stand-up comedian and played it straight. "What's up, Zara?"

"I've got my first driving lesson tomorrow. I want to be prepared."

I nodded and smiled. "I'm still saving up for my lessons."

"Are you worried?" Zara asked.

How do I answer? Should I agree with her and say I'm also a little freaked out? Or do I play it cool and say it's no big deal. "Whatevs." I shrugged. *That was an idiot thing to say.*

"I don't know how you stay so calm, Ed." Zara tapped the countertop with her purple nails. "I'm a nervous wreck."

"You don't have to be," I said, meeting her gaze. "It's not like it's the first time you've ever been in a car."

"You're right. I drive around with Tyrone all the time. I guess I should pay more attention to what he's doing behind the wheel."

I gave Zara a half smile but didn't really want her to pay any more attention to Tyrone than she did already. "I have a better idea than watching Tyrone." I scratched my chin as if I'd been seriously thinking about it for a while. "Why don't you keep your eyes on the road when he's driving?"

Zara thought about it for a second and her eyes brightened. "I can always count on you for good advice, Ed."

I handed Zara the Coke and her receipt. "Good luck studying."

Zara flashed a smile and gave a quick wave. "Later, gator!" Then she walked out of the store to her mom waiting in their car.

Standing in a daze, I replayed the words Zara had just said to me. "*I can always count on you, Ed.*" I smiled to myself. Maybe Zara might actually like me. Then I looked down. *Uh oh.* There on the counter was Zara's driver handbook. *I'm sure she'll notice she's forgotten it and will be right back.*

★ ★ ★

An hour later there was still no sign of Zara.

"See you tomorrow, Ed," Bruno said. He pointed

at the clock as it ticked closer to nine o'clock. "It's not busy tonight so why don't you take off a few minutes early?"

"Thanks, Bruno." I hurried to the back of the store carrying Zara's handbook. I slipped the precious cargo into my backpack and saddled up on my bike. Then I switched on my light to guide me through the darkness. I pedalled the heavy beast as fast as I could, riding through yellow lights and passing slower riders as I raced along. Zara needed her handbook!

When I hit Tyrone's street I made a sharp right. I knew Zara lived only a few mansions away from his party house. I rolled up the driveway. Stopping, I leaned my bike against the garage door.

A few seconds after I pressed the bell Zara swung open the heavy oak door. Her eyes popped wide when she saw me. "What are you doing here, Ed?"

"You forgot this." I plucked her handbook out of my backpack like a magician pulling a rabbit out of his hat.

"That was sweet. Come on in for a minute." Zara waved me inside the huge marble entrance.

I gave her the handbook. "You said you were going to study tonight."

Zara sighed. "I was, but then I got distracted. There are a million social postings about the last Mustangs game and the graffiti on Tyrone's car." She held up her phone screen. "See?"

I raised an eyebrow. "It's still blowing up?"

"It's crazy." Zara nodded. "It's another game between Calgary and Westside. But this time the action is all on social, not the field. It's so big I think I'm going to write another story about it."

"I can't wait to read it," I said as I put on my helmet. I wanted to stay longer but was running out of things to say. Plus, I felt like a dork standing in her fancy entrance wearing my neon-yellow biking jacket.

Suddenly, we heard car tires squealing into the driveway and a powerful engine being turned off. A car door slammed. Rapid footsteps got closer. Then there was a loud knocking behind me. I turned around and opened the door.

"Just as I thought." Tyrone's eyes narrowed. "I was driving by when I saw that two-wheeled piece of scrap metal outside. I knew it was you, Waterboy."

Zara held up her hands. "It's not what you think, Tyrone."

"Oh, yeah? What do I think, Zara?" Tyrone crossed his ripped arms. "That this skinny weasel is seeing you behind my back?"

"It's not like that at all." Zara's eyes flashed at Tyrone. "Ed just dropped by to give me my driver's handbook that I forgot at the store. He was being nice. Which is more than I can say for you."

Tyrone's nostrils flared like an angry bull. "Well, I don't like it. I don't like you talking to other guys."

Zara pursed her lips. "Well, that's too bad, Tyrone, because I'm going to talk to anyone I want. Besides, you have girls talking to you all the time — before games, during games, after games."

"I can't help it if girls like talking to me," Tyrone said smugly. "I'm the Mustangs quarterback."

"Well, I'm the Mustangs reporter," Zara snapped back. "I can't help it if guys like talking to me."

Tyrone clenched his jaw. "You mean guys like Waterboy."

"Quit getting mad at Ed." Zara gave me a quick nod. "He's done nothing wrong. If you want to know what's going on, just ask me."

Tyrone shot me an angry look. "I can see what's going on."

"No, you can't, Tyrone." Zara folded her arms across her chest as well. "Because there's nothing going on. Ed and I are just friends. That's all."

Tyrone took a step toward me and the door. "Out of my way, helmet-head. But from now on, if I was you, I'd watch my back. You never know who might be following when you're riding that piece of junk you call a bike." Tyrone looked at me coldly as he stormed outside.

Tyrone slammed the door behind him, leaving Zara and me alone again. My throat went dry. "I should be going too," I croaked over the sound of squealing rubber in the driveway.

Special Delivery

Zara gave me a friendly glance. "Thanks again, Ed. I'll see you at the next Mustangs game."

I waved goodbye and walked toward my bike. Just friends. That's all. I knew it was crazy to think Zara would want to be more than friends. Why would she? I was just a tall, skinny geek who was barely on the football team. The exact opposite of Tyrone. I shook my head — not at Zara or Tyrone, but at myself.

15 Hospital PASS

"Offence against defence!" Coach Taylor shouted at practice the next day. "The Westside rematch is coming up this Friday. They'll be coming at us hard." Coach paced in front of the team. Everyone's eyes were on him. "I understand they weren't very happy about losing the last game against us."

"You got that right, Coach," Sanjay said. "They even spray-painted Tyrone's car."

"I heard about that." Coach grimaced. "I'm sorry that happened. But we have to focus on the game. And that means playing a scrimmage. We have to practise the plays we're going to use against the Rams." Coach tossed the football to our star quarterback. "Run through our playbook, Tyrone. Make sure everyone touches the ball."

"Huddle up, offence!" Tyrone called out. "Handoff to Levi."

After taking the snap Tyrone flipped the ball to the stocky running back. Levi ran up the middle for five yards before being brought down.

Hospital Pass

In the next huddle Tyrone called a pass. "Square-out to Sanjay." This time Sanjay cut to the sideline and caught the ball. Slowly but surely we moved down the field. Each time Tyrone switched the type of play. Run . . . pass . . . run . . . pass. It wasn't long before all our key players had a play called to them. All our players except one.

Coach Taylor blew his whistle and jogged out to the huddle. "I said everyone touches the ball, Tyrone." Coach looked straight at me as he spoke to our quarterback.

"Every player has," Tyrone said.

"Not everyone," Coach said. "What about Ed?"

Tyrone narrowed his eyes. "He's no player, Coach. He's the waterboy."

"I don't know what's going on between you two." Coach put his hands on his hips. "But I want you to throw to Ed, too. He's part of this team."

Tyrone was steely-eyed. "Okay, Coach, if that's what you want."

"Yeah, that's what I want, Tyrone."

The offence huddled up again. Tyrone glared at me and called a play. "Slant across the middle to Ed."

Sanjay's head popped up. "We never call that play, Ty. That's a hospital pass, man."

"Yeah, well, we're calling it now." Tyrone clapped his hands to break the huddle.

I ran to my position on the far-right side of the line

of scrimmage. I wondered what a hospital pass was. Maybe it was a play that was only used in emergencies. Like if we were losing. But I didn't have time to think about it.

Tyrone called for the ball and took the snap from centre. I took off. First, I ran a few long steps straight ahead and then slanted toward the middle of the field. I looked up and a bolt of fear shot through me. Running toward me was our biggest linebacker. Marcus Jones was half my height but twice as wide. He was like a runaway freight train barrelling straight at me. The faster I ran, the faster he ran. I turned back toward Tyrone and looked for the pass. The ball was in the air. I reached out to grab it. But the ball never made it to me.

Smash!

I was hit by our hulking linebacker. Marcus didn't just tackle me. He flattened me. I fell to the ground like a dropped barbell. Everything hurt. My shoulders ached. My arms throbbed. My legs felt like a giant bruise. But I had a bigger problem than all the pain — I couldn't breathe. I lay on my back with no air going into my lungs. It felt like someone was trying to smother me. Like someone had a hand over my mouth.

"You okay, Ed?" Sanjay asked. He looked down at me. His eyes were wide. His face was wild with panic.

I gasped. I couldn't talk. I shook my head.

Hospital Pass

Sanjay knelt beside me. "Just try to breathe, man."

I thought I was going to pass out. Then I felt a bit of air flow into my lungs. Then a bit more. Finally, I took a deep breath. Oxygen filled my chest.

Another face appeared next to Sanjay's. "You had us scared, Ed," Coach Taylor said. "But you just had the wind knocked out of you. Your face was white as a ghost. You look better now."

I got up on one knee. "Take a break," Coach said. "Sanjay will help you to the bench."

I wrapped an arm around Sanjay's shoulder and he started to walk me off the field. We eased our way by the huddle. Coach Taylor was pointing a finger at Tyrone. "What were you thinking?"

"I don't know what you're talking about, Coach." Tyrone shrugged like it was no big deal. "I threw the ball and Waterboy got tackled trying to catch it. Happens all the time."

"That was a hospital pass and you know it." Coach was mad. "Any receiver would have been hurt running that slant into the middle. Even Sanjay."

Tyrone threw up his hands. "So what?"

"We only have two receivers." Coach stood nose-to-nose with Tyrone. "We can't afford to have one of your teammates getting hurt. Especially before our big rematch against Westside."

Tyrone looked at Coach grimly. "Only one receiver is a teammate. Only one has earned his place on the team. Only one guy can be trusted on the field, or off." Tyrone glared at me, then walked away.

Still feeling woozy, I made it to the bench and slumped down. I looked down the sideline and saw the fuzzy shape of someone walking toward me. The person slowly came into focus. It was a girl.

"You don't look so good, Ed," Zara said.

I tried to sit up straight. I didn't want Zara to think I couldn't take a hit. But even though I had been working out with Lamar I still wasn't strong enough to take such a hard tackle. I don't know if anyone would have been. "I'll be all right." I smiled bravely.

"I hope you'll be ready for the Westside game on Friday." Zara looked concerned.

"Me too," I said. But I wasn't sure hope would be enough.

16 Follow THAT CAR

I limped down the hall.

We had just finished practice and Tyrone and Zara were walking ahead of me. They were holding hands and heading for the front entrance of the school. They must have made up. I guess my dropping off her hand-book wasn't that big a deal, after all.

Zara stopped and waited for me. "Why don't you walk through the parking lot with us, Ed?"

Tyrone glared at me at first. But then he looked at Zara and nodded. It looked like he was still getting used to his girlfriend talking to anyone she wanted to.

"That's okay," I said. "You guys go ahead." I knew they were going to drive home in Tyrone's car and wouldn't want me around.

"The bike rack is just past Tyrone's Mustang," Zara said to me. "You have to go this way anyway."

I hobbled a few more steps and caught up.

"You still look sore." Zara eyed my slow-moving legs.

"I'll be okay once I get on two wheels," I said. "It'll be easier to bike than walk."

Zara glanced at Tyrone and me. "You guys are going to be interested in the story I'm writing for tomorrow's *Mustang News*. It's about the Westside rematch."

"Have their fans calmed down since the last game?" I asked.

"I don't think so." Zara shook her head. "I'm still seeing a lot of posts online. The Rams would love to steal the next game from us."

"Never going to happen," Tyrone said smugly. "Not as long as I'm playing."

We walked along the pavement toward Tyrone's hot car. He usually parked at the end of the parking lot, but it still wasn't in view.

"It's a good thing you're giving me a ride home, Ty," Zara said, fumbling with the pile of schoolbooks in her arms.

"I'll unlock the door to make it easier for you." Tyrone reached into his jeans pocket to grab the key fob for the car.

Then he stopped cold.

"I was sure I put it in here." Tyrone dug into his pocket again. Then he checked all his other pockets. "I can't find it! The fob must have fallen out when I jumped out of the car this morning. I remember being late and running to my first class."

"I'm sure everything is fine, Ty." Zara put a comforting hand on Tyrone's arm. "The key fob is probably just lying on the seat."

"But if it is, anyone could drive the car away!" Tyrone blurted. "I have to find out."

Tyrone sprinted through the parking lot to where he had left his car that morning. Zara and I hurried behind him. When we caught up to Tyrone, his arms were flung in the air.

The Mustang was gone.

Tyrone's head spun left and right. His eyes flashed with shock. "My car's been stolen!"

Zara's hand shot out. "There it goes!" She pointed at a green car speeding out of the parking lot.

"I'd run after it, but I'd never catch them." Tyrone turned to Zara. His eyes were wide. "How am I going to get my car back?"

I'd never seen Tyrone like this before. He always knew what to do on the football field. He never got rattled, no matter what. I racked my brain. I had to think of a solution.

"Ed, you've got to do something!" Zara pleaded. Tears were welling in her eyes.

Tyrone wasn't a friend. But he was the Mustangs quarterback and my teammate. If he was ever going to throw another pass my way, he had to trust me. "I have an idea."

I knew I couldn't run faster than Tyrone. But I

could pedal faster. I strapped on my helmet and staggered the few steps to my bike. Then I pulled out my phone and snapped it onto my handlebar mount. After tapping 9-1-1, I hopped on.

"This is 9-1-1," a man's voice said. "What's your emergency?"

"I'd like to report a stolen car," I gasped. My legs were already churning as hard as they could.

"Can you give me a description of the stolen vehicle?" he said.

"Green Mustang with license plate QB12," I shouted into my phone. "Last seen heading west from the Calgary High parking lot!"

The Mustang roared away. Clouds of blue smoke billowed from its spinning tires. The smell of burning rubber filled the air. I had to keep the car in sight. I forgot about the pain and stomped on my pedals.

"A police unit is on its way," the 9-1-1 man said. "Until then keep us updated from a safe distance."

"Copy that." I didn't know if I was supposed to say that. But that's what they always said on the police shows I watched on TV.

The Mustang was a block ahead of me, zigzagging through traffic. I raced behind it, dodging parked cars as I flew down the street. Suddenly, the taillights of a taxi in front of me flashed red. The car was stopping! I jammed on my brakes and swerved around it. Sweat dripped down my face. Pain shot through my burning legs. I didn't know if I could ever catch up. But I had to try.

The Mustang bolted around two more cars and was now speeding two blocks ahead. I was losing them! I put my head down and pedalled as hard as I could. When I looked up I saw that I was getting closer. The Mustang had stopped. It was rush hour in Calgary. They were stuck in a traffic jam!

Cars were at a standstill. Horns were honking. No one was moving an inch, except me. I was passing everything on wheels. Cars, taxis, buses, dump trucks — I raced by them all.

Tyrone's car didn't stay still for long. The Mustang pulled out of the long line and squealed around the next corner, just missing an oncoming pick-up truck. I put out my arm to signal a turn and hung a sharp left as well. The light was yellow but I blasted through the intersection anyway. I had no time to stop.

"Suspect is now driving south on Elbow Drive!" I yelled into my phone to relay the latest location of the getaway car. "Wait a minute, now they're turning right!"

I wasn't going to let them get away. I imagined myself as some super spy like James Bond chasing the bad guys. My legs spun faster.

I shot past a *WELCOME TO WESTSIDE* sign. *That's where they're going*, I said to myself.

"Suspects may be headed to Westside High!" I called out.

The Mustang banked sharply to one side as it

blasted around the next corner. Then it shifted into a higher gear and roared away. I made the turn toward Westside High and kept the car in sight. It was about a dozen cars ahead of me.

For the first time I heard a siren wailing. Red and blue lights flashed as a police car raced by, passing the line of cars ahead. The Mustang started to weave in and out of traffic, trying to get away. Soon the police cruiser was right on its tail. The stolen green car made one more dangerous turn and screamed toward Westside High. The cop car stayed with it.

I followed a short distance behind. Less than a minute later, the two cars sped into the Westside school parking lot. I could hear the loud screeching of tires. When I pulled in, I saw long black skid marks trailing behind both cars on the pavement.

The Mustang's driver and a passenger leaped out and started to run. But they were quickly tackled by the two cops who had chased them down. A minute later, the two car thieves were being led back to the squad car in handcuffs.

They looked about my age. I guessed they were probably the same Westside students who had spray-painted Tyrone's Mustang. The weird online threat suddenly made sense. If Westside couldn't steal a game, they'd steal a car from Calgary High. And Tyrone's dropped key fob meant they could swipe not just any car — the quarterback's.

"Suspects have been arrested," the 9-1-1 voice said.

"Copy that. Thanks." I hung up my phone and took a few deep breaths. My heart still pounded. My legs ached. My face was covered in sweat.

Pedalling home, I thought about the chase. I was glad Tyrone would get his Mustang back. I didn't know if he'd trust me more or not. But at least he wouldn't have to worry about his car. He had a big game to play. He had to focus.

17 CAUGHT

The war of words was heating up. I knew there were still lots of dumb postings on social about the graffiti sprayed on Tyrone's car. And now that his Mustang had been stolen, things were only going to get worse. I wanted to read Zara's new story and get the latest.

Taking advantage of a spare period between Math and English, I shuffled into the library. I searched for a free computer and a comfy chair. My legs were still tired from the car chase the day before. And I didn't sleep well, either. Riding home, I had heard a vehicle pull up behind me. My heart had jumped when I thought it might be Tyrone. But it had turned out to be one of those brown UPS trucks making a delivery to the house next door.

Inside the library I felt safe hidden among all the books. I didn't think Tyrone or Fish would ever set foot in the place. Zara wouldn't be there, either. She always did her writing in the *Mustang News* office.

Spotting an open screen, I sat down and put my

water bottle on the table beside me. Being the newest guy on the team, I made sure to follow all of Coach's rules, and always had my water bottle with me. A couple of clicks later I was on the Calgary High website.

I leaned forward and started to read.

REMATCH IGNITES BAD BLOOD BETWEEN SCHOOLS
By Zara Kapoor, Calgary High Mustangs Reporter

It's going to be a showdown. This Friday our Calgary High Mustangs go head to head again with the Rams from Westside. And we all know what that means — fireworks.

The action on the field will be lighting up the scoreboard. Led by star quarterback Tyrone Jackson, the Mustangs will try to overpower the Rams defence like they did in their first game. "We're the number one team in the league," Jackson told this reporter after a recent practice. "No one can stop us."

With first place on the line, excitement is already building for the rematch. The Mustangs are undefeated this year, while the one loss the Rams have suffered was against our boys in green. The winning team will have home field advantage in the playoffs, not to mention bragging rights.

Long Bomb

There could be as much action off the field as on. After the last game, Jackson made some comments that riled up the Westside fans. He said the Rams couldn't "steal a game" from the Mustangs even if it was handed to them. There were some heated words and scuffling on the field between the fans of the two teams.

There's no love lost between the two schools. Proof came after the last game, when Jackson's prized Mustang had graffiti sprayed on its side. And just yesterday the same car was stolen. But the big quarterback is taking it in stride. "This is what happens when you're the best player, playing on the best team."

League officials are taking safety for the next game seriously. "There will be extra security to make sure all the players and fans are safe. We don't want a repeat of what happened last time."

Buses leave for Westside after the last bell on Friday. Let's get out there and cheer on our team. *Go-Mustangs-go*!

My eyes were on the last line of the story when I heard two sets of footsteps coming up from behind. Tyrone and Fish thumped down on chairs, one on either side of me. Tyrone stabbed a finger at my screen. "You're at it again, bro." His voice sounded strained. "We come in here because our English teacher is making us write some stupid book report. And who do we find? Waterboy, that's who."

Fish nodded. "Yeah, Waterboy."

Tyrone went on, his voice hoarse. "Every time I see you, Warnicki, you're either talking to Zara, reading a story by Zara or doing something to impress Zara. I know that's the only reason you chased after my stolen car. You're on my turf, bro. And you better back off."

Fish nodded again. "Yeah, you better back off."

"You hear what I'm saying?" Tyrone's voice was now a raspy whisper. He struggled to swallow then stood up. His fists were clenched. His muscular frame loomed over me.

I was just about to tell Tyrone it was all a mistake when I spotted trouble coming our way.

"Hey, guys, I'm surprised to see you in here." Coach Taylor smiled.

"Book reports," Tyrone said, barely able to speak.

"Sounds like you need a drink, Tyrone," Coach said.

Tyrone's eyes widened. Coach had caught him without his water bottle!

"Good thing you have yours with you." Coach nodded at the water bottle on the table.

Tyrone met my eyes. His face was filled with panic. He knew I could rat him out. But I blinked once to give him a sign. I wanted to let him know it was okay.

"Yeah . . . good thing." Tyrone slowly picked up my water bottle and took a swig.

"That's why I have that rule," Coach said. "It's important to carry a water bottle with you at all times. You never know when you'll need to rehydrate."

"No, you never know." Tyrone's voice was strangled.

Coach fixed his gaze on me. "But I'm surprised at you, Ed."

"Sorry, Coach. I left my bottle in my locker."

"Even though you're the newest guy on the team, I have to treat you like every other player."

"I know that, Coach." I nodded. "It won't happen again."

"It better not." Coach gave me one last warning look, then turned to leave. "See you at practice, boys."

Tyrone put down my water bottle without even glancing at me. "Let's go, Fish."

I watched silently as Tyrone and Fish slinked away between the bookshelves.

18 Taking a LAP

Practice had just started. We were all circled around Coach Taylor at midfield. His hands were on his hips. He looked stern.

"You know I have a lot of rules," Coach said. "You have to listen to what I say in the locker room. You have to do what I say on the field. And you have to carry a water bottle with you during your school day." Coach paused as he scanned our faces. "Well, I'm sorry to report that one of you let me down on the last one. Someone didn't have a water bottle with him this afternoon."

Every head looked around, wondering who got caught. Every head turned but mine.

"And you all know what the penalty is for not having a water bottle with you?" Coach asked.

Every head nodded. "Laps."

Coach pointed a stubby finger at me. "Okay, Ed, get running. Ten laps of the field."

Surprise rippled through the team. "I can't believe it's you, Ed," Sanjay said. "You're the last guy to do something like this. You always have a water bottle. You're the waterboy."

I strapped on my helmet and started jogging to the edge of the field. I ran slowly, knowing I had a long way to go. Trying to make it easier, I took long strides. But my legs were still sore. They ached from being tackled and were tired from chasing down the carjackers on my bike. I felt a little wobbly and stumbled a couple of times.

"Ed doesn't even run like a human," Levi laughed. "He runs like a giraffe."

"Or like he's on stilts," a big lineman called out.

"I'm sure glad no one else has to do laps," Sanjay said. "That would wear out anyone for the next game against Westside."

Suddenly, there was an uproar among the players.

"Hey, Tyrone!" Coach shouted. "Where are you going?"

I turned to see what Coach was yelling about. The big quarterback was running straight for me. *He must still be mad at me for reading Zara's story*, I figured. My muscles tightened getting ready for the hit . . .

"Thought you might like some company," Tyrone said as he pulled up beside me.

I looked at him with surprise. "You don't have to do that."

Tyrone gave me a quick glance. "Yeah, I think I do. I owe you, bro."

"It's no big deal," I said, taking another long stride.

"Why didn't you tell Coach, Ed?" Tyrone asked. "Why did you take the blame? It was your water bottle, not mine."

"It's simple." I shrugged. "I did it for the team."

"What do you mean?" Tyrone asked. He was taking two steps for every one of mine.

"Because you're more important to the team than I am. I'm just a second-string receiver. But you're the quarterback. You're the leader of the team. The other players look up to you. They can't think you did something wrong. They can't think you don't follow the rules, because then no one would."

Tyrone ran a few more steps before he spoke. "I never thought of it that way. You think about the team more than I do."

"Coach can't think you did something wrong, either," I said. "He's got to believe in you. He's got to know you won't make mistakes on the field. That you'll always make the right call."

"I try to," Tyrone said.

"I know you do." I nodded. "You're the best QB in the league."

I thought Tyrone might thank me for not busting him to Coach. Or for tracking down the car thieves. That he might think I wasn't just a tall, geeky guy in a uniform that didn't fit. But he stayed quiet as we ran together for a few more strides.

Finally, I broke the silence. "Besides, it's better that I get tired out from running laps before the next game than you. You have to make sure Westside doesn't steal the game from us."

I glanced over at Tyrone. I wasn't sure but I thought I saw the hint of a smile.

"Tyrone, get back here!" Coach shouted. "You have to save yourself for the Westside game."

Tyrone sprinted back to the rest of the team in the middle of the field. I kept loping around the sidelines. Nine laps later I was done. And so was the practice. While the rest of the team was preparing for tomorrow's game against Westside, I was running. I had missed the whole thing. I grabbed a water bottle and jogged back to join the rest of the squad as they were wrapping up.

Coach Taylor clapped his thick hands together. "Okay, Mustangs, let's bring it in."

We formed a tight circle around him. Coach reached out and put one hand in the middle of the giant huddle. "Mustangs on three!" he shouted.

"One . . . two . . . three . . . Mustangs!" Tyrone shouted. Sanjay shouted. Marcus shouted. Everyone shouted.

The team was ready for the Westside game the next day. I just hoped I was too.

19 Visitors IN BLUE

The next morning I was back in the school parking lot. I put my wheels in the bike rack, shouldered my backpack and headed inside to my locker.

After running all those laps, I was hoping to have just another boring day of classes at Calgary High. I needed to save my energy for the big rematch. I rounded the corner and stopped dead in my tracks. Tyrone and Fish were waiting for me at my locker.

I froze like a statue. Was I walking into a trap? I knew not everyone wanted me on the team. Maybe Tyrone was going to tell me not to play in the big game this afternoon.

Tyrone waved me closer. "I've got something to say to you, bro." His face was serious.

"Yeah, something to say," Fish repeated.

I took a few steps nearer. My hands started to sweat.

"When I discovered my Mustang had been stolen, I couldn't believe it." Tyrone locked eyes with me. "But then you hopped on your bike and chased down the car thieves. And that's not all. You called the police at the same time. I'm not sure I could have done it."

"Yeah, not sure," Fish said, sticking his face in mine.

Tyrone shot Fish a look. "Give us some space, wouldya, bro?" Fish's oily face grimaced and he moved away.

"Then the cops brought my car back all in one piece. They told Zara and me how you helped them catch the thieves." Tyrone gave me a nod. "You can read all about it in the *Mustang News*."

I relaxed. Tyrone wasn't out to get me. "There's a story in the *Mustang News*?" I asked. "About me?"

"Sure is," a girl's voice said. "A great story, as usual."

Zara had just come out of a classroom. "Hey, Z," Tyrone said as he pulled her to his side. "Why don't you read a bit for Ed?"

Zara tapped her phone a few times until the story flashed on her screen. "Here's the headline and first paragraph." Zara started to read in her reporter's voice.

"CAR THIEVES TRACKED DOWN BY STUDENT HERO. Not all the action was on the football field Thursday afternoon. While the Mustangs were practising, getting ready to steal another game from the Westside Rams, another theft was taking place on the streets of our city. Tyrone Jackson's green Mustang was stolen in broad daylight from our school parking lot. His car might have disappeared forever if not for the bike-riding heroics of Mustangs teammate, Ed Warnicki."

Zara lowered her phone. "And that's just the beginning of the story."

Tyrone patted me on the back. "I've been wrong about your wheels, bro. Sometimes it is better to have a bike than a car."

Just then, the sound of heavy footsteps came thumping down the hall. Two burly police officers in their blue uniforms were marching toward us. We could see their holstered guns and hear the jangling of handcuffs attached to their belts.

"We're looking for Ed Warnicki." The policeman's voice was stern and official.

My heart started to pound. Were the cops here to arrest me? Maybe I had made an illegal turn while I was chasing Tyrone's car on my bike. Maybe that yellow light had turned red. I got ready for the cuffs to be slapped on my wrists and for me to be hauled away.

"I'm Edward Warnicki," I croaked. I used my full name, thinking it would soon be appearing under my mug shot.

"I'm Sergeant Miller and this is Sergeant Adams," the biggest of the two cops said. "We've come by to thank you for your bravery earlier this week, Ed."

"To thank me?"

"We never could have caught those two car thieves from Westside," Sergeant Adams said. "If it wasn't for your quick thinking and excellent bike riding skills."

Sergeant Miller reached into his pocket. "We'd like to thank you in a more meaningful way, as well."

"You don't have to do that," I said, expecting a handshake.

"We always give out a Crime Stoppers reward for any information leading to the arrest of car thieves." Sergeant Miller handed me a white envelope. "I'm pleased to present you with this cheque for a thousand dollars."

I could hear Fish gasp. "You're kidding," I said, my eyes popping wide.

"No, the money is all yours. It's what happens when citizens like you do the right thing." Sergeant Adams smiled. "Have a rewarding day, Ed."

The two policemen turned and marched away, their heavy boots echoing down the hall.

There were a few seconds of silence when no one knew what to say. Everyone was in shock, including me.

"This is a great story," Zara said. She pulled out her reporter's pen and notebook. "What do you think you'll do with the money, Ed?"

I knew what to say right away. "Looks like I'll be able to pay for those driving lessons sooner than I thought."

"And if you have any money left over, I have a suggestion for you." Tyrone pointed at my feet. "Get some new cleats, bro. Your days of wearing clown shoes are over."

The bell rang. We all had classes to go to. But I knew we'd all be thinking about the big game after school.

Tyrone reached out to bump fists with me before he left. "Let's hope you can catch passes as well as you catch car thieves."

20 Double COVER

"This is the rematch we've been waiting for."

Coach Taylor stood on the sideline giving us last-minute instructions. We were about to take the field against the Westside Rams. "Remember the game plan. On defence we have to stop their running attack."

"Go, D!" shouted Marcus, the big linebacker that had cut me in half in practice.

"On offence we have to mix up our running and passing games," Coach said. "On the ground, Levi and Carlos have to grind out some yards."

Levi and Carlos pounded fists.

"And when we pass," Coach said, "Sanjay will be Tyrone's number-one receiver."

"I'll get the job done." Sanjay nodded.

"If Sanjay can't get open, we'll throw to Ed." Coach glanced my way.

Snickers spread through the team.

"Why would Tyrone ever throw to Ed?" a big lineman asked. "That's just a wasted pass."

Long Bomb

I lowered my head. I was getting better in practice. I was getting stronger in the weight room. But no one seemed to care. I wondered if anyone besides Sanjay and Lamar wanted me on the team.

Tyrone took a step toward the big lineman. "I'll tell you why, bro." Then he cast his eyes around the whole team. "I'll tell you all why. I don't just pass to receivers who have a lot of talent." Tyrone nodded at Sanjay. "I pass to receivers I trust. Guys that may not be as fast, but guys that I know will do whatever it takes to make the catch. Guys that will sacrifice everything for the team." Tyrone looked my way. "Guys like Ed."

Even though I was the tallest guy on the team, I knew not every player looked up to me. But if Tyrone was on my side, that was enough. I raised my head and stood up straight.

★ ★ ★

This afternoon's game was on the Rams' turf. But our fans were in the stands already shouting at the top of their lungs. I watched Zara take a few snaps of our cheerleaders dancing on the field.

We've got the spirit. Come on, let's hear it. Go Mustangs!

Calgary High students weren't our only fans in the crowd. Mom had driven Mildred over to the game. I saw her sitting in the stands. I just hoped she wasn't sitting beside Tyrone's parents telling them to turn down the music at their next party.

The football fell through the sky like a meteor hurtling toward earth.

The crowd roared as the Rams return man caught the kick-off on his own ten-yard line. He sped straight up the middle of the field for twenty yards before one of our linebackers could bring him down. The grudge rematch had begun.

I sat on the bench with Lamar, who was still hurt. We watched the action with the rest of the offence. I was nervous. My leg bounced up and down as I waited for my first chance to get in the game.

The Rams were marching down the field as if they had something to prove. Their running attack was coming at us in waves. Their powerful fullback was built like a steamroller. He flattened us on almost every play. His thick legs pumping like pistons, it wasn't long before he plowed through our defensive line for the first touchdown of the game. The Rams took the lead, 7–0.

This wasn't how Coach Taylor wanted the game to start. He paced back and forth in front of the bench like a caged tiger. "Let's get it back, offence!" he shouted. "Okay, Tyrone, get out there!"

I followed the green uniforms onto the field and joined the Mustangs huddle. I stood at the back, looking over the heads of my teammates. Tyrone stood in front of us and called the first play. "Post to Sanjay."

I relaxed, knowing Sanjay was the primary receiver.

Long Bomb

The pass wouldn't be coming my way. I didn't really expect many balls to be thrown to me this game. Sanjay was Tyrone's go-to guy. We just needed another receiver on the field. Someone the Rams thought could catch a pass. Someone like me.

A Westside cornerback covered me as I loped down the field and stopped after twenty yards. I shot a glance over at Sanjay, who had sprinted straight down the sideline and cut toward the goalpost. From there, he reeled in Tyrone's pass for a big thirty-yard gain.

Back in the huddle Tyrone called our second play. "If it worked once, it'll work twice. Post to Sanjay."

At the snap of the ball, I ran downfield again. But this time something was different. I didn't see anyone covering me. The Rams cornerback had decided I wasn't worth watching and had run over to double-cover Sanjay. Tyrone released a perfect spiral, but Sanjay was sandwiched between two defenders. He wasn't in the clear. The second Rams cornerback leaped high and picked off the pass. He tucked the ball under his arm and scampered back to our forty-yard line.

"I was double-teamed," Sanjay complained as he ran up to Tyrone.

Tyrone nodded. "They figured out that you're our number-one receiver. They think Ed is just a decoy. They don't think I'll ever throw to him."

I followed Tyrone and Sanjay back to our bench. The Westside fans were on their feet cheering the interception: "Steal! Steal! Steal!"

Coach didn't waste any time coming straight over to Tyrone. "We have to change our game plan. Now that two guys are on Sanjay, he's never going to get open."

"What about throwing to Ed?" Tyrone asked.

Coach glanced my way and pursed his lips as he thought. "Let's try running the ball first."

The new game plan started to work. When we had the ball, Tyrone started making hand-offs to our two running backs. Levi and Carlos took turns running dives, counters and draws. They shot through gaping holes in the Rams defence almost every down. After five plays, Levi blasted over the goal line for a touchdown. The ref's arms shot high over his head. The game was tied, 7–7.

After we kicked off, Westside mounted another long attack. The Rams moved down the field like an army. We were the enemy and they were invading our territory. They got as close as the thirty-yard line before our defence could shut them down. Marcus made a bone-cracking tackle to stop their drive. The Rams tried a long field goal for three points. But at the last second the ball hit the goalpost and fell to the ground. We had dodged a bullet.

Tyrone led us onto the field. We had one more chance to score before the end of the first half. We huddled up at centre field. "Draw to Carlos," Tyrone called out.

The ball was snapped. Tyrone took a few steps back to fake a pass. The Rams surged across the line, thinking they were about to tackle the quarterback. But

Long Bomb

Tyrone handed the ball to Carlos at the last second. The Rams had been fooled. There was a big hole where the linemen should have been. Carlos was short and stocky with good wheels. He darted through the gap in the defence and sprinted upfield. He juked left and right, leaving a trail of fallen Rams on the ground. No one could tackle the shifty running back. Finally, the speedy Rams safety shoved Carlos out of bounds at the one-yard line. It was an incredible run.

There were only a few seconds left, but Tyrone knew what to do. "Dive to Levi," he called out in the huddle.

We lined up on the Rams one-yard line. We were so close we could almost taste the touchdown. Tyrone grabbed the snap. Levi came charging from behind him. Tyrone handed him the football and Levi jumped. He soared through the air, diving for the goal line.

The Rams were a smart team. They knew what kind of play was coming. They had stacked their defensive line with extra players to stop the run.

As Levi sailed through the air, a big Rams linebacker took off to meet him head-on.

Crunch!

You could hear the tackle all over the field. Levi tried to hold onto the ball. But the pigskin popped out of his arms and rolled along the grass. A Rams player dove for it. A Mustangs player dove for it. But the Rams player pounced on the ball first.

Double Cover

The referee blew his whistle once. "Rams ball!" Then he blew it again. "End of the first half!"

We had come so close to taking the lead but had fumbled on the goal line. The score was still Rams 7, Mustangs 7. The game was headed for a second-half showdown.

21 Hands UP

Coach gave a short pep talk as we grabbed drinks from the table.

Even though I was playing I still had some water-boy duties. Before the game, I made sure we had plenty of cold water for the afternoon. I may not have been able to fill in for our all-star receiver Lamar, but I could fill a water bottle like a pro.

"We almost had another touchdown," Coach said. "That proves our running game is working. Let's keep it going!"

For most of the second half Coach was right. Tyrone continued to hand off the football to Levi and Carlos. And the two running backs kept pounding out first downs. We weren't able to score, but we made it deep into the Rams zone. The game was all going according to plan — until we fumbled again. Carlos was hit hard and the football squirted out of his fingers like a watermelon seed. Westside pounced on the loose ball at their twenty-yard line. That's where the team in blue started their long march toward our goal line.

Play after play, the Rams picked their way down the field. A run, a pass, a sweep — our defence tried everything but couldn't find a way to stop them.

The long Westside drive ate up the clock. By the time the Rams running back darted into our end zone, there was less than a minute to play in the game. The only good news was that one of our big linemen was able to stop their convert after the touchdown. He reached up a beefy hand and blocked the kick for the single point. I glanced at the scoreboard: Rams 13, Mustangs 7.

This doesn't look good, I thought.

"We still have a chance!" Coach Taylor shouted. "We can do this, Mustangs!"

Tyrone snapped on his helmet. He charged back onto the field. I raced behind him with the rest of the offence. The ball was on the Rams fifty-yard line after an awesome kick-off return. But it was time that was the enemy now. We had only forty-eight seconds to score.

First play, Tyrone handed the ball to Levi. *Bam!* Levi ran around the right end for ten yards. Second play, Tyrone flipped the pigskin to Carlos. *Pow!* Straight up the middle for ten more. We made two first downs and were on the move. Now we were on the Rams thirty-yard line. But time had almost run out. There was only one second left on the clock.

Tyrone raised his hand and called for a huddle. We gathered in front of him. "We only have time for one play," he panted.

"Who's getting the hand-off?" Levi asked.

"No one," Tyrone said.

"But Coach wants us to run the ball," Carlos said.

"They'll be expecting another run." Tyrone shook his head. "Plus, it's still thirty yards to the goal line. We need to pass."

Tyrone remained calm. He scanned the faces in the huddle. I expected him to stop when he got to Sanjay. He was our number-one receiver. But he kept going and locked eyes with me. "Can you get open, Ed?"

I stared at Tyrone like a zombie, not able to speak. *Last play of the game and Tyrone wants to pass to me?* "Yeah, I think so." I nodded. "They've been covering Sanjay, not me."

"Corner to Ed on two," Tyrone called out.

"Can you even throw it that far?" I asked. "That's a fifty-yard pass."

"I don't know." Tyrone clenched his jaw. "But a long bomb is our only chance."

I looked at Tyrone one last time. "Make sure you throw it to me high."

At the snap of the ball I ran downfield as fast as I could. I didn't care what people thought of me. How gangly my legs looked. How my skinny arms flailed. I wasn't loping like a giraffe — I was galloping like a Mustang.

Hands Up

I kept sprinting downfield. When I hit the goal line, I cut for the corner of the end zone. Then I looked back. Tyrone had already launched the pass. The ball flew through the bright blue sky. It was spiralling straight for me.

I knew Tyrone was counting on me to catch the pass. But I wasn't just catching it for Tyrone, or for Sanjay or for Lamar. They all believed in me. This time I was catching the pass for myself. I could do this.

"The pass is too high!" Coach shouted from the sideline. "Ed will never catch it!"

Suddenly, the Westside defenders who had ignored me all game came charging. The ball sailed toward me. I raised my arms way over my head. Higher than I ever had before. The two Rams players jumped. They tried to knock down the pass. But neither one was tall enough. Neither one could reach that high. Tyrone's pass was perfect. The ball hit my outstretched hands and I squeezed. Squeezed as tight as I could. Squeezed like I was at the park playing with my dad. I pulled the ball down and held it tight against my chest. Nothing was going to make me drop it. I fell to the ground, a twisted pile of arms and legs.

The first sound I heard was the referee blowing his whistle. *Touchdown!* The second sound was Tyrone standing by my side, saying, "You did it, Ed! You did it!"

22 Game BALL

The team bus drove us from Westside back to Calgary High. We charged off the bus holding our helmets in the air. We had kicked the convert after my touchdown and won the game by a single point. Whooping and hollering, we ran into our locker room. The party to celebrate our big comeback against the Rams was about to begin.

Coach Taylor stood at the front of the locker room and raised his arms. When the wild cheering had died down, he said, "As you know, it's a Mustangs tradition to award a game ball to the game's most outstanding player."

Sanjay, Lamar, Marcus and the rest of the team began chanting: *Game ball! Game ball! Game ball!*

"Well, today we have two outstanding players." Coach held up two footballs, one in each of his big hands. "The first is our quarterback."

The players started chanting again: *Tyrone! Tyrone! Tyrone!*

Game Ball

"Yes, Tyrone Jackson." Coach nodded at his star quarterback. "What a pass! I don't think anyone thought you could throw a football that far. And that included me."

Tyrone grinned at Coach. "I didn't know I could throw a long bomb that far, either. But I had to. It was the only way we could win."

"It was the longest pass I've ever seen in a high-school football game," Coach said. "And that the throw came on the last play of the game made it even more impressive. For that, you deserve this game ball." Coach patted Tyrone on the shoulder pads as he handed him the first football.

Coach held up the second football in front of the team. "But a long pass only gives you a chance at victory. To win the game someone has to catch that pass. Catch it in the end zone for a touchdown." Coach looked my way. I was standing in the far corner, my usual spot after games. "Today, that someone was Ed Warnicki."

I didn't think my name would ever be chanted. And certainly not by the Mustangs football team. But that's what I was hearing. Every player was shouting my name. Even Tyrone was yelling: *Ed! Ed! Ed!*

I could feel my face turning red. But not because I was embarrassed. For the first time I was proud of who I was. Proud to be tall. Proud to be skinny. Proud to know other players thought I deserved to be on the team. I pulled back my shoulders. Now I was standing up — for myself.

"When I saw Tyrone throw the ball, I didn't think there was any way Ed could catch it." Coach shook his head in disbelief. "The pass was way too high for almost any receiver to grab. But Ed is no ordinary receiver. He's a receiver with big strides, big hands and a big heart. Nothing was going to stop him from catching that ball. Nothing was going to stop him from winning the game for the Mustangs." Coach walked past every player in the locker room and handed me the second football. "For Ed's amazing catch, he deserves a game ball as well."

The team started chanting my name again and didn't stop until I sat down.

After we showered and got dressed, Tyrone and I walked out of the locker room together. Zara was waiting in the hall. But she wasn't alone.

"This is my friend Lucy," Zara said. "She wanted to meet the stars of the game."

"Both of you guys are heroes." Lucy beamed. I don't know if I was seeing things, but she seemed to be smiling more at me than at Tyrone. "That last catch you made was unbelievable, Ed." She *was* smiling at me! Suddenly, being "just friends" with Zara didn't seem like such a bad thing.

"Why don't we all go to 7-Eleven for a Slurpee?" Zara suggested.

"My treat," I said, as we headed across the parking lot toward Tyrone's car.

"Great idea." Tyrone dangled his key fob. "Hop in, everyone."

"Where are you going, Ed?" Lucy asked, as I walked past the car and got on my bike. "I was hoping you'd come with us."

I smiled. "I'll meet you there."

"Don't be too long." Lucy smiled back.

"Don't worry about my man Ed," Tyrone laughed. "With his wheels, he'll probably beat us there."

ACKNOWLEDGEMENTS

Just as in football, it takes a team to get a book ready for the big game. *Long Bomb* would never have taken the field without Lorimer's publisher Carrie Gleason and editor Kat Mototsune. Their coaching helped me create strong characters and ensured I didn't fumble the ball when it came to the storyline. Assisting on the sideline was Susmita Dey, the production editor whose care and attention are evident in the handiwork you hold in your hands.

I'd also like to send out a fist bump to fellow writer Kyle Herron for his knowledge of all things automotive. A final thanks goes to my wife and two tall sons, who allow me to revisit the high-school years with such great memories.